Elizabeth Laird

Elizabeth Laird was born in New Zealand but she lived in London until she grew up. As soon as she could, she began to travel, and went off to live first in Malaysia, then in Ethiopia, Iraq, Lebanon and Austria. Now she lives near London with her husband, who is also a writer, and her two sons. She likes reading (a lot), gardening, walking, going to the cinema, talking to friends and cooking (sometimes). As well as *Kiss the Dust* she has also written *Red Sky in the Morning* (Highly Commended for the Carnegie Medal), *Hiding Out* (winner of the Smarties Award) and *Secret Friends*. Her most recent novel for Mammoth is *Jay*.

Kiss the Dust

Elizabeth Laird

EGMONT

First published in Great Britain 1991
by William Heinemann Ltd
Reissued 2001
by Egmont Books Ltd
239 Kensington High Street, London W8 6SA

Text copyright © 1991 Elizabeth Laird
Cover illustration copyright © 2001 Steve Rawlings

The moral rights of the author and cover illustrator have been asserted

ISBN 0 7497 4932 6

10 9 8 7 6 5 4 3 2 1

A CIP catalogue record for this title is available from the British Library

Printed and bound in Great Britain by Cox & Wyman Ltd,
Reading, Berkshire

*This book is dedicated to
the refugees of Kurdistan*

Preface

The Zagros mountains are like a long spine of high peaks. They start in the north at the eastern end of Turkey and go southwards, separating the plains of Iraq in the west from Iran in the east.

About twenty million Kurdish people live in the foothills of the Zagros and in the fertile valleys that lie between the high peaks. The international borders of Iran, Iraq and Turkey run right through the Kurdish areas, so there are millions of Kurds in each of the three countries.

The Kurds have lived in the Zagros mountains since history began. Although they are Muslims, they are not the same people as their neighbours, the Arabs and Persians. They speak their own Kurdish language, wear Kurdish clothes, tell their own stories and have their own customs and traditions.

The Kurds do not have a nation state of their own. They are ruled by others, by Turks in Turkey, Arabs in Iraq, and Persians in Iran.

At the end of the 1970s, fighting broke out between the Kurds of Iraq and the government of Saddam Hussein. The *pesh murgas*, as the Kurdish fighting men were called, fought successfully at first for a homeland of their own.

But the Iraqi government's response was ruthless. They bombed and gassed Kurdish villages, executed Kurdish fighters and their families and completely destroyed many Kurdish towns and villages. Thousands of refugees escaped across the mountains to Iran.

But by this time, Iraq was at war with Iran, and to the Iranians, Kurdish refugees were enemy aliens. The

Iranians couldn't let people from an enemy country settle wherever they wanted to in Iran. They sent the refugees to remote camps in the deserts of the south or the mountains of the north.

This is the story of one Kurdish family. The people in this book are not real, but their story is like that of thousands who have been forced to run away from Iraq across the Zagros mountains.

1

It was just an ordinary day like any other. Tara and her friend Leila, dressed like everyone else in uniform navy skirts and pale blue blouses, walked out of the big gates of the Secondary School for Girls in the centre of town, swinging their heavy school bags. It was that short time of year between the icy cold of a northern Iraqi winter and the blasting heat of an Iraqi summer when the sky is a melting cloudless blue and every plant seems to be in flower.

"Don't let's go straight home," said Leila. "I want to look round the shops."

Tara hesitated. Her mother was strict about her getting home in reasonable time.

"I'm not sure," she said. "Daya gets worried if I'm late."

"Oh, come on," said Leila. "Your mother won't notice if it's only ten minutes. And you can get something for Hero."

"Good idea." Tara linked her arm through her friend's and swung her bag up onto her shoulder. Her three year old sister Hero had chicken pox. It was hard work keeping her amused. A packet of

1

crayons or something might keep her happy for a while.

The main road that led to the centre of Sulaimaniya wasn't usually very busy, but today it was choked up with a lumbering convoy of army jeeps and lorries that churned up clouds of dust. Tara and Leila hardly noticed them. Since the war with Iran had started four years earlier, they'd got used to seeing the army everywhere. They shouted to make themselves heard above the roar of the heavy engines.

"What did you get in your English test?" said Leila.

Tara made a face.

"Bad marks as usual. I don't think Mrs Zeinab likes me. She's always getting at me. I think she's mean."

"She's not really," said Leila earnestly. Tara squeezed her friend's arm. It was just like Leila to stick up for Mrs Zeinab. She never criticized anyone. She was so softhearted she'd feel sorry for a flower when its petals started to drop.

"I'm hopeless at English anyway," said Tara. "It's so difficult. And we've got miles of irregular verbs to learn for homework. I'll never do it."

"Yes, you will. I bet you know half of them already."

"I bet I don't."

"No, honestly. Go on. I'll test you. Um . . . *bite*."

"*Bite*, er, *bit* . . . oh, I don't know. *Bited*?"

"No, *bitten*."

"See what I mean?"

"Try another. *Break*."

"*Break, broke,* — *broken*!" recited Tara triumphantly.

"Brilliant! You see? You do know them Some of them anyway. *Bring*."

"*Bring, bringed* . . . Hey! Watch out!"

The last truck in the convoy had slowed down and got left behind. It suddenly roared up to close the gap, swinging dangerously close to the side of the road.

"It nearly hit us!" said Leila angrily.

Tara didn't answer. She had jumped back right under a branch of richly scented blossom that was dangling over a high garden wall. She was breathing in lovely gusts of perfume. They seemed to go to her head. She reached up, picked a spray of flowers and tucked it into Leila's buttonhole.

"Go on," she said. "Sing a song. You know, like Najleh Fathee in 'Springtime'." She clasped her hands together on her chest and rolled her eyes up to the sky.

Leila giggled.

"Stop it!" she said. "You are awful. Someone might see us!"

The usual crowd of midday shoppers were out and about in the streets of Sulaimaniya. A group of children was gathered round the entrance to the pastry shop, looking longingly at the sticky piles of honey cakes set out on trays in the window.

Three very correct ladies, unrecognizable under

their all-covering black veils, were looking at the contents of the vegetable seller's baskets, pinching the tomatoes to see if they were firm, and discussing the price of potatoes.

On the corner of the street, the tea house was already full of men, talking business over their tiny glasses of hot sweet tea, and shooting backgammon pieces backwards and forwards on the boards.

Outside the mosque, four high school boys stood clustered round a friend, who was excitedly reading to them from a paper he held in his hand.

"Let's go over to old Mr Faris's shop," said Leila. "I should think he'd have something for Hero, and he might have some new film posters in too."

Tara was about to plunge across the street in her usual impetuous way, when the quiet of the town was once again shattered. Two army jeeps, horns blaring, came screeching down the road and squealed to a stop outside the mosque. A dozen soldiers, rifles in hand, leaped out.

Afterwards, Tara could see the whole scene as clearly as if it were a film still unrolling in front of her. The shocked faces of the shopkeepers, peering out from their doors, the children by the window full of sweets, the huddle of veiled women, the men in the tea shop, their glasses in their hands, the turbaned mullah who had appeared in the doorway of the mosque, the four boys in their crisp white shirts, the paper they had been reading fluttering to the ground.

What happened next seemed as unreal as if it really was a film. A short nervous looking officer marched across to the boys. He shouted an order. One of them bent to pick up the paper he'd been reading and gave it to the officer, who held it between his thumb and forefinger as if it might infect him. Then he tore it up, dropped it, and ground it under his foot.

He stepped back, and shouted an order. The soldiers ran forward, two men to each boy, grabbed them by the arms and pressed them against the wall of the mosque. The officer seemed to have lost control of himself. He was almost screaming.

"Enemies of the state! Spies! Shoot them!"

The soldiers looked round at him uneasily. The officer yelled again.

"Are you disobeying orders? Shoot!"

Four of the men knelt in the dust and raised their rifles to their shoulders. The mullah, his green cloak flapping round him, ran out of the mosque gate, waving his arms helplessly.

"No! No!" he shouted. "Stop! They're only boys! Don't shoot!"

The officer fumbled at the leather holster in his belt with shaking fingers. He pulled out his revolver, pointed it at the bewildered mullah, and fired.

At the sound of the shot the whole street seemed to flinch. Tara and Leila clutched each other, hardly able to believe their eyes. The mullah, his cloak billowing out round him, sank to his knees and toppled forward into the dust, groaning, and clutching his shoulder.

The boys suddenly made a dash to escape. They darted free of the soldiers' grasping hands, and seconds later had disappeared round the corner of the mosque into the next street. But one of them, the boy who had been reading from the paper, wasn't fast enough. A soldier's outstretched foot tripped him up. He fell sprawling in the road. The officer dashed up, and stood over him. Helplessly, the boy looked up, and saw the look in the officer's eyes.

He raised a clenched fist.

"I die for Kurdistan!" he shouted. The sound of a shot ripped deafeningly through the air. The boy jerked convulsively, his arms and legs twitched, and then he lay still.

In the awful silence that followed, a crow left its perch on the minaret and flapped slowly down to settle above the gate of the mosque.

The officer, still brandishing his revolver in the air, turned to face the ring of terrified faces that watched him from every corner of the street.

"Look!" he shouted. "Look at this traitor! I'm warning you, anyone who helps the Kurdish rebels will die like him, only it will be more painful! Look at his blood! Go on! Stare at him! Don't forget, any of you!"

As suddenly as the jeeps had burst into the street they had gone. At once everyone ran forward to the wounded mullah and the dead boy, lying in the dust. Tara shut her eyes. She didn't need to look. The whole scene was printed on her mind. She didn't need that stupid officer to tell her not to forget it. She never would. She never could. In all her life she'd never seen anything so brave as the way that boy had died.

She found she was trembling. Her knees felt weak. Beside her, Leila was sobbing. Tara suddenly felt terrified. She pulled at Leila's arm.

"We've got to get out of here quickly," she said. "They might come back!"

She found she was too trembly to walk, then the strength seemed to come back into her legs, and holding Leila's arm she started to run. A few minutes later they were back in their own familiar street.

"Why?" panted Leila, tears still streaming down her cheeks. "Why? Why?"

Tara gritted her teeth. Leila might be the kindest person in the world, and brilliant at English, but she wasn't clever at all when it came to the big things, like the way people behaved, and the reasons why they did things.

"You know why," she said. "That boy was a Kurd, like me."

"He must have been in league with the rebels, I suppose," said Leila doubtfully.

"They didn't bother to stop and ask before they shot him, did they?" Tara said furiously. "And anyway, the pesh murgas aren't rebels. They're freedom fighters!"

Leila walked on in silence.

"You don't understand anything, do you?"

Tara said. "The Kurds . . ." she stopped. It was no use. There was no point in discussing it with Leila. She was an Arab, although she had a Kurdish granny. Whether you were Kurdish or Arab hadn't bothered the two of them much until today. Suddenly it seemed the most important thing in the world.

They had reached the big double gates that led into Leila's garden.

"See you tomorrow," Tara mumbled, and ran next door into her own house.

2

Tara's mother, Teriska Khan, was sitting in the kitchen cross-legged on a cushion, coaxing Hero to eat. She looked up in surprise as Tara burst in through the door, threw down her bag, and then dropped down onto the rug beside her, and burst into tears.

"What is it? What's happened? What on earth's the matter?"

Tara shook her head. She couldn't say anything. Hero tore off the table napkin tied round her neck and pushed her bowl away. She wasn't very hungry, and anyway, she didn't want Tara interrupting her lunch. She liked having her mother all to herself.

Tara picked the napkin up and tried to tie it round Hero's neck again.

"No! Ow! You're hurting me!" Hero wriggled out of reach, and looked crossly at her. Then she grabbed the napkin and gave it to her mother. "Daya do it! Daya put it on!"

Teriska Khan settled her back into her place on the cushion, tied the napkin again and popped a piece of banana into her mouth.

"Be quiet, Hero. Eat up your lunch. Come on, Tara. What's happened? Just tell me."

Tara blew her nose.

"Oh, Daya, it was so awful, you wouldn't believe it. Leila and I went to the shops after school . . ."

Once she'd started talking, Tara couldn't stop. The story poured out of her. And when she'd told it once, she found herself beginning all over again. Though she'd stopped crying, she still felt shaky all over. She just wanted to talk, and talk, and talk.

"It was so horrible! You can't imagine! It was so awful, I just felt stunned."

"Yes, you must have done," said Teriska Khan. Tara looked at her in amazement. Her mother looked shocked and horrified, but she didn't seem especially surprised by what had happened. She was shaking her head and making sympathetic noises, but all the time she was chopping bits of banana up for Hero. It was as if Tara was telling her a story she'd heard before.

Tara started to feel irritated.

"You don't understand, Daya," she said. "It might have been Ashti! They were his age or even younger! Only sixteen, some of them, I'm sure." At the thought of her brother, she suddenly sat bolt upright.

"Where *is* Ashti, anyway?" she said. "Shouldn't he be at home by now?"

Teriska Khan started clearing away Hero's lunch dishes.

10

"He went into Baghdad this morning with your father. They'll be home late tonight. Ashti doesn't need to go into school every day, now that he's finished his exams."

She looked at Tara thoughtfully.

"I'm sorry you saw that today," she said. "We've tried to keep you out of it all. We wanted you to have as happy a childhood as possible before . . ."

"Childhood!" interrupted Tara indignantly. "Daya, I'm nearly thirteen!"

"I know you are, darling, and I suppose we've protected you for too long."

"Protected me from what?"

Teriska Khan stood up, and began to clear away Hero's dishes.

"From what's going on," she said. "From what's happening to us Kurds."

"What do you mean?"

"We've tried to keep you out of all the politics. The arrests and executions. The pesh murgas fighting the government. It's been much worse since the war with Iran started. The secret police are everywhere. They're scared of Kurds, even of boys like the ones you saw today. They hate us because they're scared."

"Hate us? You mean the Arabs hate us? Leila's an Arab. She doesn't . . ."

"Of course she doesn't, darling. I said the government hate us, not ordinary Arab people. There are millions of Arabs in this country who've got no more reason to love this government than the Kurds have. Some have even less in fact."

Tara didn't usually find her homework especially difficult. She and Leila often worked together. Leila helped her with Arabic and English, while Tara tried (mostly unsuccessfully) to help Leila understand maths. Tara was good at maths. She liked to worry away at a problem until the solution untied itself like a knot coming undone.

Tonight it was different. Leila didn't come, and Tara was glad. She had too much on her mind. She felt scared. The war had been going on for years but it hadn't touched her somehow. She'd heard explosions in the night sometimes, and shots, and Kurdish girls at school had talked in whispers about relatives who'd disappeared, or news they'd heard about the fighting in the mountains, but she'd never really got involved. She'd known all sorts of things were going on. You couldn't live in Iraq and not know. But she'd shut her mind to it all. She hadn't wanted to think about it. It would be different now though. Seeing that boy die had made all the difference. She couldn't shut her mind to things any more.

She sat in front of the TV in the big comfortable family sitting room, fiddling with the gold stud in her right ear like she often did when she was worried. Her parents should have told her more. They shouldn't have treated her like a little kid. She was a Kurd too. She had a right to know what was going on. Anyway, she liked thinking about serious things, about people being brave and noble and heroic. At least, she liked them in stories.

Suddenly she saw the boy's head lying on the pavement, with the bullet hole in it. She shuddered. Perhaps heroism wasn't all that great in real life. It was too quick and brutal and casual.

The programme was finished. Tara hadn't taken in a word. The news came on. She tried to concentrate. She hadn't bothered to follow it very closely up till now. There was a clip of the President at a military parade, and a lot of loud music. It was funny, she'd never noticed it before, but every news programme showed the Iraqi army winning, and hundreds of Iranians being killed or taken prisoner. But if the Iraqis were always winning why hadn't the war ended years ago?

She got up and switched the TV off. The house was unusually quiet tonight. When Ashti was at home he made enough noise for ten, even if none of his friends was visiting. And her father usually had several callers in the evening, who could be heard arguing and discussing in the formal sitting room near the front door that was reserved for Kak Soran's guests.

The air-conditioning hadn't been switched on yet. In a few weeks' time, when the blistering summer heat arrived, its continuous low hum would blank out any sound from the dark garden and city streets outside. But tonight Tara was vaguely aware of the noises of the cool spring evening. There was a distant rumble of cars and lorries from the main streets of the town. A loud, crackling radio was blaring out music from some open window not far away.

What was that?

Tara's head jerked up. It sounded like shots. She'd often heard shooting after dark before, but Daya had always said it was just trigger happy soldiers taking pot shots at stray cats. And there wasn't only shooting either. Every dog in Sulaimaniya seemed to be barking. And the greyhound next door, that always scared her stiff when she went past the gates, was the loudest of all. She turned off the light, went over to the window and peeped out through the heavy black-out curtains.

The moon had come up. It made the garden look all silvery and unreal. The big hound next door sounded absolutely frantic now. It was jumping up against the dividing wall, rattling its chain and barking its head off.

Surely something else was out there? Tara peered forward, trying to see into the deep shadows by the wall. She was sure something had moved under the shade of the old almond tree. Yes! There it was again!

Tara gasped and opened the curtain wider. There *was* someone there. He was bent double now, running from the almond tree to the big clump of bougainvillia beside the kitchen door. A strange man! In their own garden! It could be a thief, or even a murderer! And her father and

14

Ashti were away in Baghdad. She and Daya and Hero were all alone.

"Daya!" shouted Tara, running out of the room. "Daya! Come here! There's a thief in the garden!"

Teriska Khan came racing out of her bedroom.

"Are you sure? Quick! Bolt the back door!"

They were too late. They burst into the kitchen to find that the man was in the house already.

He was tall, lean and deeply sunburnt. He wore the baggy trousers, tight jacket and sash of a mountain Kurd. A turban was tied round his head and the fringe dangled over one eye. His left arm was roughly bandaged with a bloodstained rag, and the long loose sleeve was torn right up to his shoulder. He carried a deadly looking rifle in his right hand, and he was just putting it down on the table when Tara and Teriska Khan dashed into the room.

When he saw them, the mouth under his drooping black moustache split open into a friendly smile, and he suddenly looked younger.

"Hello, Teriska," he said. "And who's this? Surely it can't be Tara? If it is, she's grown a lot since I last saw her."

Teriska Khan ran forward.

"Rostam!" she said. "They've hit you! Oh, my God, however did you get here? Tara, go to the medicine cupboard in my bedroom, and get some lint and a bandage. Your uncle's wounded."

3

Tara pushed open the door that led to the narrow corridor at the back of the house off which the three bedrooms ran. Hero was standing by the door of her parents' room. Her face was flushed, her eyes were puffy and her nightdress was trailing on the floor. She coughed, and Tara saw that her nose was running.

"What are you doing out of bed?" Tara said. "I thought you were asleep."

"I am asleep," said Hero indignantly. "I was in the toilet. I want a drink. If I don't have a drink I'll wake up. And I'll start crying, and . . ."

Tara picked her up. The mysterious uncle in the kitchen was probably bleeding to death. There was no time to waste on Hero. But nothing on earth would shake her once she'd got an idea into her head. If she wanted a drink she'd make sure she got one, or she'd scream the house down for it. And a screaming Hero was the last thing they needed tonight.

She pushed open the door of her parents' bedroom, and put Hero on the big double bed. Hero lay back and began to finger the pink frill on one of her mother's pillows.

"A drink," she said, and an ominous whining undertone started to creep into her voice. Tara looked round anxiously. She didn't want to go back to the kitchen. Hero would probably follow her, and then the fat would be in the fire.

Then she saw a tray on her mother's bedside table. Thank goodness! There was a jug of filtered water and a glass on it. She poured some out quickly and gave it to Hero, who took a couple of sips, then, to Tara's great relief, lay back on the pillows.

"Nice," she murmured, fiddling with the fringe again, while the thumb of her other hand crept towards her mouth. Tara watched her anxiously for a moment. Hero's eyes slowly shut. The eyelids flickered as if she was trying to open them again, but the effort was too much for her. She was obviously asleep.

Tara slowly let out her breath, and tiptoed over to the big cupboard opposite her parents' bed. What was it Daya had wanted? Lint and bandages? There they were, on the second shelf. She'd take the lot while she was about it. She wouldn't be surprised if the whole kitchen had filled up with wounded men by the time she got downstairs again. The world had turned topsy turvy. Anything might happen tonight.

Teriska Khan met her at the kitchen door.

"Did I hear Hero?" she said. "Is she awake again?"

"No. She's gone back to sleep. She only wanted

a drink. I didn't tell her anyone was here."

"Good. We'd better keep her right out of this. She's much too young to keep a secret. She'll have to see Rostam in the morning, but she mustn't know he came secretly in the night, and she mustn't know he's wounded. You've got to remember that, Tara. No one must know, not Leila, not the neighbours, not any one at all. There mustn't be a hint, or even a look. If it got out that we're sheltering a wounded pesh murga, who's wanted by the police, God knows what . . . It's a matter of life and death for all of us."

"Yes, Daya." Teriska Khan had never talked to Tara quite like this before. She sounded so serious, as if she was talking to another grown-up. Tara was nearly as tall as her mother now. She pulled herself up to her full height. Teriska Khan was looking straight into her eyes, as if she was looking for something there.

"It's all right," Tara said. "I really do understand. You can trust me, you know."

Teriska Khan smiled.

"I know I can, darling. You've got the bandages? Good. Take them into the kitchen. The wound's deep, but I don't think the bone's damaged. I forgot to tell you to get the disinfectant lotion too. I know exactly where it is. I'll go and get it myself."

Tara stood outside the kitchen, screwing up her courage to go in. She'd never met this uncle before. She hardly knew of his existence. The only men she was used to were her father and Ashti.

18

Other men, unless they were close cousins, never got past the guest sitting room near the front door. They certainly didn't go into the kitchen and perch on the table, as this uncle had done. After a long moment, curiosity got the better of her, and she opened the door.

The kitchen was big, but Tara had the strange impression that her uncle filled the whole of it. It was so odd to see an unfamiliar man in the room. He was half sitting on the table, his short woven coat removed and one shirt sleeve rolled right up to the shoulder. On any other occasion, Tara would have felt completely tongue-tied, but the wound in her uncle's arm, the bloody clothes on the floor, the bowl of red water and the gory smears on the pristine whiteness of the formica table made everything seem so extraordinary that she found her tongue at once.

"Shouldn't you go the the doctor?" she said anxiously.

Uncle Rostam didn't even seem to be aware of the horrid red pulp on his arm. He laughed, and his teeth showed strong and white in his sunburned face.

"Doctors might talk, little niece," he said. "Even Kurdish ones. Your mother's a good enough doctor for me."

"But who are you? What happened? Who shot you?"

He raised his eyebrows.

"I'm your Uncle Rostam. I'm a pesh murga. One of 'those who face death'. Didn't you know?

Or has my cautious city brother kept me a secret from his children all these years?"

He laughed at the expression on her face, but the extra movement made him wince. He put his left hand up to his upper right arm, and Tara could see a strip of cloth tied so tightly above the wound it seemed to be biting into the muscle.

"Oh, be careful," she said. "Look, it's started bleeding again."

Helplessly, she watched the trickle of blood thicken as it ran down her uncle's sinewy arm, then feeling a bit faint she looked away as Teriska Khan came back into the kitchen, a bottle of lotion in one hand and a pair of scissors in the other.

"Keep out of the way," she said to Tara, "and don't touch anything. We don't want the wound to get infected."

She went to the sink to wash her hands, and caught sight of a chink where the curtains hadn't been properly pulled. "Pull them across tightly," she said to Tara, drying her hands. Rostam chuckled softly.

"Hiding a fugitive's a serious crime, sister-in-law," he said through gritted teeth as Teriska Khan began mopping up the blood with a piece of sterile lint. She didn't answer but frowned down at the mess on his arm.

"Do you think the bullet's still in there?"

"I – don't – know," he said through clenched teeth. "I don't think so."

Tara couldn't look. She felt rather sick. How

could Daya bear to poke and probe at it like that? And how could Uncle Rostam be so brave?

"I'm sure there's nothing there," Teriska Khan said at last, straightening up. "But it ought to be looked at by a doctor. It really needs stitching."

"No! No doctors! No hospitals!" Rostam jumped off the table and stood, swaying slightly. Teriska Khan shook her head, but didn't say anything. She dabbed some disinfectant ointment onto a dressing, put it gently on the wound, and tied a bandage round it. Then she loosened the tourniquet above the wound.

"What about your old friend, Dr Mohammed Bakir?" she said at last. "He wouldn't betray you, or any other pesh murga. I know he wouldn't."

"No!" Rostam backed away from her, towards the door. "That's just where they'll look first, at all the doctors' places. They know they hit me. The police are out like flies, buzzing all over Sulaimaniya. They must have had a tip-off from someone. They obviously knew we were getting a shipment through tonight." He frowned suddenly at Tara, and stopped talking. She frowned too. Uncle Rostam obviously thought she was just a little girl who couldn't be trusted. He probably thought she was scared of a bit of blood too. She'd show him.

Swallowing hard, she picked up the bowl of red stained water and threw it down the sink. Then she steeled herself to pick up the bloodstained clothes from the floor, and took them over to the sink too. She turned the tap on, and began to rinse them out.

"If they had a tip-off . . ." Teriska Khan said quietly, and stopped. Tara turned to look at her. Her mother didn't usually say much, and Tara was used to reading her thoughts. Uncle Rostam seemed to do so as well.

"They won't know I've come here, I'm sure they won't," he said. "No one saw me after I got away from the checkpoint on the Chuarta road. There's no reason why they'd look for me here."

"Did they know it was you? Did they recognise you?"

"I don't think so."

For the first time, Tara saw a shadow of doubt, a flicker of anxiety cross her uncle's bold, confident face. Into the silence fell the distant, threatening whine of a police siren.

Teriska Khan picked up the scissors and the unused lint.

"Well, we'd better get ready, just in case," she said briskly. Tara felt her skin prickle with fright. She wanted to jump into the nearest cupboard, shut the door, and cower in the dark.

How could Daya be so calm and brave? Tara had seen her cope with disasters before, like when Hero had been sick in a taxi, all over the driver, or when Ashti had collected millions of grasshoppers and let them loose in the kitchen, or when Auntie Suzan had been in that terrible car crash, but now here she was, practically operating on a serious gunshot wound, and proposing to hide a wanted man from the secret police.

Teriska Khan turned Tara round, and propelled her towards the door.

"Get on with it," she said in her usual matter-of-fact voice. "Take this bloodstained cotton wool and flush it down the toilet. And don't leave it until you're sure it's all gone. I'll get Rostam some clean clothes. Ashti's shirts will be too small for him, but one of your father's might do. Then when you've got rid of the cotton wool, come back to the kitchen and get every tiny bloodstain washed away."

"Yes, Daya," said Tara, trying not to mind how bloody her fingers were getting as she picked the bits of saturated lint off the table. "But what'll we do if they do come? Where can you hide him?"

"I'm not going to tell you," said Teriska Khan. "The fewer people who know the better. Now, don't worry. They're not likely to come here after all."

A few months earlier, Tara's father, Kak Soran, had paid a fortune to have the kitchen completely done up. Tara never went into it without admiring the polished marble floor, the dazzling white paintwork and the rows of electrical gadgets. But tonight, for the first time she missed the old kitchen, with the brick coloured tiles that used to be on the floor, and the old wood effect formica surfaces.

No one had had the sense, when they were planning the new kitchen, to think how impossible it would be to clear away the evidence of a wounded man. It was easy enough to wipe a cloth over a drop of blood on the shining stainless steel sink, but even after several tries, you could still see the smear left behind. And however hard Tara scrubbed and rubbed at the stains on the floor, she couldn't seem to make the freshly washed part look exactly the same as the rest of it, which her mother had gone over that morning. It just looked different. And when she thought she'd finished, and got rid of every trace, she found a whole new set of bloody red fingerprints on the back of the chair which her uncle had been gripping while Teriska Khan was cleaning his wound.

Tara was just working over these when she heard something that made her flesh come up in goose bumps. A car was coming down the quiet street towards the house. They were here! They'd come for him! And she and her mother would be arrested too, tortured perhaps, even shot! She couldn't move. She felt rooted to the spot. Then she remembered something her father used to say to Ashti.

"A Kurd never shows he's afraid," he'd said.

Tara took a deep breath, and forced herself to make a final cool inspection of the kitchen. She was just about to rush out when she caught sight of her own hands. There was a red streak on her own wrist! Her heart gave a sickening lurch, and she darted to the sink to wash it off. Then she heard the car stop outside the house, and one, then another door slam, and she tore off to warn her mother.

Teriska Khan was coming out of the bathroom, wiping her hands on a towel.

"What's the matter now?" she said.

"Daya! There's a car! It's stopped outside. There are people getting out. I heard the doors slam!"

"It'll be Soran I expect. I thought he'd be home hours ago," said Teriska Khan. "Is the kitchen finished? And you've got rid of the cotton wool? OK. Now in case it's not your father, remember, no one's been here all day except for your cousin Latif who called earlier this evening. When he realized your father hadn't come back from Baghdad, he went away again. Got that?"

She'd hardly stopped speaking when a man's voice called out,

"Teriska, Tara – where is everyone? I've got a surprise for you."

Tara felt she was waking up from a nightmare. Her father was home at last.

"Baba!" she shouted, and ran towards the front door.

Kak Soran had put down his brief case and was unwinding the scarf from his neck. He grinned broadly at her.

"You all seem very quiet this evening," he said. "Don't tell me Hero's asleep already? What's the matter with you? Look who's here!"

He stepped sideways, and Tara saw, beside Ashti, a short person all dressed in black, from the scarf that completely covered her white hair to the hem of her ankle length dress.

"Granny!" she said, and ran over to give her a hug.

Everyone was talking and laughing at once.

"I had no idea . . ." said Teriska Khan.

"Well," Granny said comfortably, "Soran finished his business early, and came to see me, and said why didn't I come up here for a week or two, and Suzan seemed a lot better, and said she could do without me for a bit, so I thought I would. He only gave me half an hour to pack my things though." She still had her arm round Tara, who was breathing in the well remembered smell of camphor and cinnamon that always seemed to cling to Granny's clothes.

"What's for supper?" said Kak Soran, striding towards the kitchen. "It's been a long drive."

"Oh! Oh, good heavens!" said Teriska Khan. "I forgot all about your supper!"

"What?" Kak Soran looked astonished. He was used to a perfectly run household, to an endless supply of beautifully ironed shirts, and delicious meals ready whenever he wanted to eat. In all the years they'd been married, Teriska Khan had never forgotten to cook his supper before.

"We have been rather busy this evening," said Teriska Khan apologetically. "You see . . ."

Tara suddenly collapsed into giggles.

"Busy?" she spluttered, feeling almost hysterical with relief. "*Busy?* Yes, I suppose you could call it that. You could say we've been busy!"

4

Tara always felt awful first thing in the morning. She was sleepy and snappy, and she couldn't usually face talking to anyone until she'd washed her face and drunk several glasses of hot sweet tea from the samovar in the kitchen.

But today was different. She'd woken up with a funny feeling in the pit of her stomach, a sort of excitement with a nasty kick of terror in it. Then she'd rolled over and seen the humped shape in the bed by the window that Hero usually occupied. Of course! Granny was here!

She jumped out of bed as yesterday came flooding back. In record time she'd washed and got dressed. She'd brushed her long soft curly hair and pinned it back with her favourite pink hair slides, and she was in the kitchen ready for breakfast.

Uncle Rostam was sitting on the rug at the far end of the room by the window, leaning against a cushion. Beside him, mixed up with the ordinary jumble of breakfast things, was his revolver. It looked all wrong there, like a poisonous snake in a bouquet of flowers. His cartridge belt was on the floor too, the bullets almost sticking into the butter. He'd taken off the sling which Teriska Khan had made for his wounded arm. He obviously couldn't be bothered with it.

Ashti was sitting on the floor beside him. He seemed to have forgotten all about his breakfast. He was listening so hard to Rostam he wouldn't have noticed if the house was on fire. His thick dark hair, which he was usually rather vain about, and brushed carefully into place before he appeared in the morning, was flopping uncombed over his forehead.

"Go on, uncle," he was saying. "What did you do next?"

Rostam held his tea glass delicately between his thumb and forefinger, and noisily sucked in a hot sweet mouthful. Then he put the glass down and wiped his long drooping moustache with the back of his hand. Neither of them noticed Tara. She helped herself to a piece of bread and a glass of tea and slid down beside her brother.

"We ambushed them of course," said Rostam.

"How?"

"Oh, it was easy." Rostam picked up his revolver and squinted down the barrel. "That stretch of road was perfect for a surprise attack. There were ten of us strung out along the top of the cliff, and a few more in a cleft of the rock on the corner where the road zigzags down the mountainside. When the first five army trucks had gone past we let them have it. Pow! We took them completely by surprise."

Tara remembered the boy in front of the mosque and shivered. Rostam didn't notice. He was absorbed in his story.

"The ones at the end of the convoy started backing away down the road, revving up like crazy. The ones in front tried to race on and get out of it, but our lot were waiting for them at the next corner."

"Did you blow up the trucks?"

"Of course not! We needed them, and anyway, they were full of supplies for the army garrisons. You should have seen the stuff they had! Tins of oil, and sacks of flour, and sugar and fresh vegetables, coffee, cigarettes – we couldn't believe it! We'd been short of food for weeks."

"What about the soldiers?" asked Tara shyly. "What did you do to them?"

"Four or five got hit in the first attack. They were past helping. The others didn't put up much of a fight." Rostam chuckled. "You could tell their hearts weren't in it. They didn't stand a chance against us pesh murgas on our own ground, and they knew it. We didn't want to take any prisoners. They're a nuisance. You've got to feed them, and we haven't got enough food for ourselves. So we took their weapons, patted them on the head, and told them to run home to their mummies and not to come back to the mountains again or the nasty Kurds might eat them. They ran all right! Bolted off like horses! It must have taken them days to get home."

"Tara!" Tara jumped. Teriska Khan was

standing in the kitchen doorway. She sounded cross.

"What's the matter, Daya?" Tara said, surprised.

Teriska Khan fussed round the breakfast things, picking up empty plates and sweeping up the crumbs.

"You'll be late for school," she said at last. "Go and get your books. Leila's probably wondering where on earth you are. As for you – " she looked at Ashti.

Ashti wasn't listening. He had gingerly picked up Rostam's revolver, and was testing the feel of it in his hand. Tara saw Teriska Khan frown, and her eyes darted across to meet Rostam's. Tara had a funny feeling that there was some kind of battle going on between them. She didn't dare stay to see who'd win. With her mother in this mood, there was only one thing to do. Obey – at once.

Leila was waiting by her own garden gate. She'd done her hair in a new way, combed straight back from her forehead and tied at the back with a plastic butterfly clip. It made her look at least two years older.

Tara didn't even see it. Anyway, it seemed like a year at least since yesterday, when she'd gone to school with Leila on what had seemed like just another ordinary day. Yesterday she'd have noticed Leila's hair at once. Today she was too busy worrying about all the awful secrets she had to keep. She was scared that Leila might see something in her face. It was a horrible feeling. She and Leila had always told each other things.

She rushed into the story she'd agreed on with her parents.

"My granny's come to stay. And my father's cousin. Baba brought them both in the car from Baghdad last night."

Luckily, Leila didn't seem particularly interested.

"Did you tell them about what happened yesterday, with the boy, and the mullah, and everything?" she asked eagerly. "What did they say?"

"Nothing much," Tara said. She didn't want to talk about the boy. She still felt shaky every time the image of him flashed back into her mind. There was no point in discussing it with Leila. She obviously didn't feel the same. Tara tried to think of some way of changing the subject, but she wasn't quick enough.

"Wasn't it awful, though?" Leila went on, not noticing the look on Tara's face. "I nearly died of fright! I'll never forget it. I couldn't sleep a wink all night. My father says . . ."

Tara suddenly felt like boiling over.

"I don't want to know what your dad says!" she blurted out. "What does he know about it? He's an Arab, isn't he, just like that officer!"

Leila stopped dead on the edge of the road. The two of them had turned out of their street now onto the main road, where the unpaved verge was narrow, and the traffic came uncomfortably close. Leila stepped back.

"What on earth do you mean?" she said. Two bright spots burned in her cheeks. "Are you telling me you think my father's like that man?"

Tara had stopped too. She and Leila were glaring at each other.

"Well he's an Arab isn't he? Why should he care? What's it to do with him that we can't live freely in our own country?"

Now Leila was shaking with fury too.

"So that's what you think of me is it? That's the kind of friend you are! Well, let me tell you, Tara Hawrami, what my father *did* say. He said that the shooting was a disgrace, and this government are nothing but a bunch of bandits, and he can't understand why the Kurds don't have the right to organise things for themselves same as everyone else. But that's not good enough for you, is it? You think . . ."

"Leila! Look out!"

Tara dived towards Leila and in the nick of time dragged her off the road. A truck had appeared as if from nowhere, careering wildly towards them, and it had almost swept Leila under its wheels. It shot past with a shriek of its horn.

"Thanks," said Leila sarcastically, pulling her arm out of Tara's grasp. She began to walk on quickly towards the school which was now only a few hundred yards away.

Tara ran to catch her up.

"Leila, wait, listen. I must have been mad! I

didn't mean . . ."

"Didn't you?"

"No — I didn't mean you. Honestly. I just suddenly felt so angry and upset."

There were groups of girls all round them now, walking in through the school gates. In a minute they'd be surrounded by the others. It was their last chance to say anything privately.

"Look, Tara," said Leila in a trembling voice. "Don't ever say things like that to me again! Lots of Arabs hate this government and this war as much as Kurds do. My father . . ."

She stopped, and Tara suddenly recognised the look in her eyes. So Leila had family secrets too that she was trying hard to keep! Tara felt she'd been a complete fool. She chuckled unsteadily.

"My Granny's always saying that a Kurd has no friends," she said. "She's wrong about me, though. I'm really sorry, Leila. See you after school." And she ran up the steps towards her classroom.

Usually, the family ate together at lunchtime. School and office hours began early in the morning and ended early in the afternoon, and Teriska Khan liked to wait until everyone had got home before she dished up the lunch. But today she didn't seem as keen as usual for everyone to eat together.

"Your father's going to be back late from the office today," she said to Tara, turning the heat down under the pot of rice that was cooking on the stove. "Your uncle will eat with him. The rest of us can have ours now. Call Ashti and Granny, will you?"

The family sitting room was next to the kitchen. Tara opened the door. At the nearest end of the long room, Granny was playing with Hero on the big silk Persian rug.

"Tara!" Hero jumped up. "Look! I got a new dress! Granny got me a new dress!" She turned round to show herself off, and she looked so funny, all done up in a froth of white and lemon frills that Tara laughed.

"Daya says lunch is ready," she said.

She looked down to the far end of the room. Ashti and Uncle Rostam were sitting next to each other on a couple of the dark blue velvet chairs that lined the pale blue walls. Rostam looked uncomfortable. He was used to sitting on a hard floor, not on a soft chair, and anyway, his arm was obviously hurting. Ashti was leaning forward, his elbows on his knees, his chin propped in his hands. He was just as wrapped up in what Rostam was saying as he had been hours ago at breakfast time.

"Come and have lunch, Ashti," Tara called down the room to him. "Uncle, Daya says you'll want to eat later, with Baba."

Ashti looked round quickly, then turned his back on Tara.

"I'll eat later too," he said.

Back in the kitchen, fragrant wisps of steam were rising from the lamb pilau. Tara felt hungry.

She sat down.

"Where's Ashti?" said Teriska Khan.

"He says he'll eat later with Baba and Uncle Rostam."

"Oh, he will, will he?" Tara couldn't understand why Daya seemed so annoyed. Then she saw that Granny was shaking her head at Teriska Khan.

"You can't stop him," she said. "Ashti's eighteen. He's a man now. If he wants to, he'll do it. There's nothing you can do to stop him."

What are they fussing about? thought Tara. What does it matter if Ashti eats with them or with us? Then she forgot about her brother, and helped herself to another spoonful of pilau.

In the end, Ashti and Rostam ate alone. Kak Soran didn't come home till hours later. Tara was lying on the floor beside the big table in the sitting room, reading a film magazine, when all the men came into the room together. They didn't see her.

"I've managed to get in touch with several of our people," Kak Soran was saying. "They know you're here, Rostam, and not too badly wounded. They're expecting you tonight, at the usual place. And I told you about the supplies. I set all that up last week. They said they reckoned they could still get everything through."

"Baba!" Ashti sounded excited. "I thought you'd stopped being involved in politics last year, when you had that warning the secret police were after you!"

"Yes, well," Kak Soran said, and Tara could hear from his voice that he was smiling. "You were only a kid then. That's what you were supposed to think. But you might as well know now that I've never stopped working with the pesh murgas. They need city men, respectable, educated, serious men like me, just as much as they need crazy idiots like this bandit Rostam."

Tara thought Rostam would be offended, but he didn't sound it at all.

"It's true, we do need back-up people like you," he said, "but we need more fighters too. It's getting really bad up there in the mountains. We've had far too many casualties. They're stepping up the action all the time, bombing the villages, shooting anyone they catch – in the last raid on our base alone they got seventeen of us! We need more fighters, young men to train . . ."

The door opened. Tara peeped round the legs of the table. Teriska Khan had come in.

"Is Tara here?" she said.

Tara felt herself blush. It was awful to be caught eavesdropping, especially when you hadn't really meant to in the first place. But before she had the chance to come out from behind the table, Teriska Khan burst out angrily, "You've been talking about Ashti, haven't you? I'm not completely blind, you know. I can see he's dying to go off and join the pesh murgas, like all the rest of them. But I won't have it, Soran. You'll have to put your foot down. I mean, what about his place at the university? He's got his education to think about."

Tara couldn't see Kak Soran's face, but she was longing to peep out and have a look. Teriska Khan never, never talked to him like that, especially not in front of other people. She must be really upset to speak out so strongly. Tara waited for Baba to let fly. But when he did speak, it was in a patient, resigned voice that was even more infuriating than an angry one.

"Calm down, Teriska," he said. "You've got to face up to it. Ashti's call-up papers will come any day now. You don't get exemption by being a student any more so he can't go to university anyway. He's got to make a decision. He'll either get drafted into the army, and then he'll be sent off to the front to fight the Iranians, or he can go back to the mountains with Rostam and join the pesh murgas. It's got to be one or the other. You surely don't want him to get sent to the front? At least with the pesh murgas he'll be fighting for a good cause, with his own people."

Tara forgot all about being embarrassed. Before she had time to think she wriggled out from under the table.

"I would," she said, more loudly than she'd intended to. Everyone jumped.

"What were you doing under that table?" said Kak Soran, looking angry.

"I'm sorry, Baba," said Tara. "I was reading." She held up her magazine.

"What do you mean, 'I would'?" said Ashti eagerly. "You would what?"

37

"I'd join the pesh murgas rather than the army, any day," said Tara, blushing hotly. She wasn't used to expressing an opinion in front of the men of the family.

Rostam threw back his head and laughed, in a ringing voice that was better suited to empty mountain sides than an enclosed sitting room.

"Good for you, Tara!" he said. "What a pity you're not a boy! I'd have you in my company like a shot."

He saw Teriska Khan glare at him, and put up his hands to ward her off.

"Sorry, sorry," he said. "Only joking. After all, she's not a boy, is she?"

5

In the next few weeks life seemed to get back to normal for a while, on the surface anyway. But it wasn't really normal at all. At least, it wasn't like it had been before the boy had been shot, and Rostam had come. Tara wondered how on earth she could have been so blind for so long. Nothing seemed the same any more. It was as if she'd been wearing dark glasses all her life, and had suddenly taken them off.

She'd patched things up with Leila, in fact she felt even more fond of her than she had done before, though they both knew there were things between them now that they didn't dare talk about. But even though they were still good friends, they didn't want to go on doing the things they'd always done together. It wasn't much fun looking round the shops any more. It brought back too many memories. And in the evenings, when they were doing their homework, even the sound of a dog barking or a car door banging would make them jump and look at each other awkwardly.

Teriska Khan seemed different too. She was

often in a bad mood these days. Tara knew she was worried about Ashti. He'd slipped away in the night with Uncle Rostam. He'd looked so happy and excited, with his suitcase in his hand and his coat slung over his shoulder that she'd felt a funny kind of jealousy. She missed him of course, but she still couldn't help feeling angry with him. He hadn't seemed to care that Daya was crying, and Granny was nursing her cheek in her hand the way she always did when she was upset. All he could think of was the adventures he was going to have, of the fighting, the ambushes, the tough night journeys, of becoming one of the hard men of the mountains.

To take her mind off everything, Tara tried to plunge into her schoolwork. It wasn't easy. Teriska Khan had always been only too keen to make sure she had time for homework. She'd always taken an interest in her marks, and encouraged her to study hard. Now, suddenly, schoolwork didn't seem to matter any more. Even though the end of the year exams were looming, Teriska Khan kept telling Tara to shut her books and help Granny get the supper ready, or keep Hero amused, while she got on with a whole host of suddenly urgent tasks. She seemed to be busy all the time now, either endlessly fussing over drawers full of clothes, or out visiting people. No one seemed to appreciate the fact that Tara had revision to do.

"I can't think why you're straining your eyes over those books," Granny kept saying, "when you haven't even finished sweeping the floor. What will your husband think of you, if ever we manage to find one for a girl who doesn't know how to keep house properly? Girls should learn to cook, and make themselves look nice for their husbands, not ruin their eyes over books."

It was no good trying to point out to Granny that Tara had no intention of just keeping house all her life. She was going to get a degree and have a good job. She might teach Maths, like Mrs Avan, or work in a bank, like her cousin Lana. She'd get married sometime of course, but that didn't mean she couldn't work as well. Lana was a perfectly good wife, and her house was always lovely, but she managed to earn a good salary as well.

Granny would never understand all that. To her, a woman's place was in the home, and it was a family disgrace if a husband couldn't earn enough money to keep his wife in comfort.

There was no point in trying to talk to Baba either. He was never there. Since Ashti and Uncle Rostam had left he'd been busier than ever, out till all hours, backwards and forwards to Baghdad and Mosul. Tara hardly ever saw him these days, and when she did he looked tired and worried.

All in all, it wasn't at all surprising when he went down with a virus. He was up being sick all one night, and had to stay at home the next day. He simply didn't have the energy to get up.

Tara got home from school early that day. She

was in the kitchen, helping Granny to pick over the rice for lunch, when the doorbell rang.

She jumped up.

"I'll go," she said. "It's probably Leila. She promised to bring back my geography book today."

She took a short cut through the empty guest sitting room to the front door, and threw it open.

"Hello, Lei—" she began. Then she stopped, embarrassed. A man she didn't know stood on the door step. He looked nervously over his shoulder down the empty street before he spoke to her.

"Mr Soran – is he at home?" he said in Arabic.

Tara hesitated.

"I – I'm not sure," she said doubtfully. The man looked suspicious. He obviously wasn't a Kurd, and she didn't think he was one of her father's usual friends, who often came to visit in the evenings. She wasn't at all sure that he'd want to see him. She heard Granny coming to investigate, and stepped back to call to her. The man saw his chance, nipped in through the door, and shut it quickly behind him.

"Hey!" said Tara, indignantly. "What do you . . ."

Granny interrupted her.

"Do you wish to see someone?" she asked calmly.

The man mopped his forehead. Tara relaxed a little. He looked more frightened than frightening.

"I must see Mr Soran," he said rapidly. "It's very important."

'I'll see if he's at home," said Granny, sounding grand and dignified. "May I know your name?"

"Oh – yes. Just tell him Mahmoud, from the office."

Tara left him standing by the front door and retreated into the guest sitting room. She was looking round to check that everything was ready for a visitor in case Baba invited him in, when she heard Kak Soran's voice. He'd gone round to the front door through the hall, and he sounded astonished to see his guest.

"Mahmoud!" she heard him say. "Whatever brings you here? What's the matter, man? You look scared to death."

Mr Mahmoud's words came so fast they seemed to be bubbling out of him.

"They came for you, Mr Soran. Today."

Kak Soran seemed to know at once who "they" were.

"How many of them?" he said.

"Two men. They didn't wear uniforms. But it was the police. I'm sure of it. They were very polite, said it was a routine matter, not to bother to tell you they called."

Tara had intended to slip out through the door that led from the guest sitting room into the kitchen, but she found she couldn't move. She was holding a cushion she'd picked up in order to plump it up. She stood hugging it to herself.

Kak Soran said, "Why did you come here? It's

dangerous! You should have telephoned."

"I didn't dare use the telephone, sir. You never know who's listening these days. I came as fast as I could without attracting attention — left my car a block away and walked to the house. I don't think anyone saw me."

"What time did they come?"

"Ten o'clock this morning. Two hours ago. I told them you'd gone to Baghdad on business."

"They'll phone head office to check on me there."

"No, sir. I thought of that. I told them you were doing business at the bank, sorting out some tax matters. I said you had various calls of a business nature to make in Baghdad and you probably wouldn't be home until tomorrow evening at the earliest."

Kak Soran laughed shakily.

"Mahmoud," he said, "that was brilliant! I'm extremely grateful to you. If ever I could repay you, in any way . . ."

"No need. I may not be a Kurd, but I don't have any reason to love the secret police, I can tell you. May I ask — what do you intend to do?"

"I don't know. I'll have to think it over."

"Don't — don't think it over for too long. They believed me, I'm sure of it, but I've only put them off for a short while. A day at the most. They'll be after you soon."

"I know. Don't worry. I've got time enough. I hope you don't get into trouble yourself over this, Mahmoud. You've taken an awful risk coming here."

"It was nothing. It's been a pleasure to work for you, believe me. I shall miss you."

Tara heard the front door open. There was a pause as the two men looked cautiously up and down the street. Then Mr Mahmoud said,

"Goodbye, sir. And good luck."

The front door had scarcely closed behind him when Tara heard someone open the back door that led into the kitchen from the garden. Her mother had come home from a neighbour's house, where she'd been all morning.

"Teriska!" Kak Soran called. Tara heard her mother's feet come running.

"Soran! Why on earth have you got up? You ought to be in bed."

Their voices faded as they went along the passage to the kitchen. Tara put her cushion down. She was shivering. This was it then. They were in real trouble now. But the strange thing was that even though it had come like a bolt out of the blue, with no warning, she didn't really feel surprised.

"I suppose I've been sort of expecting it," she thought.

She went into the kitchen. Teriska Khan was sitting at the table, chewing her knuckles.

"I heard what that man said," Tara told her. "What's Baba going to do?"

Teriska Khan stood up and went over to the sink. She began to pile up some saucepans that had been left to dry, banging them together with unnecessary violence.

"He'll have to go tonight."

"But he's not well! He's been sick all day!"

"Try telling that to the secret police! He'll have to leave as soon as it's dark, sick or not."

"Where's he going?"

"To the mountains, of course, To join Rostam."

"How long for?"

"How should I know?" Teriska Khan snapped the cupboard door shut on the last of the saucepans.

"But Daya, we can't live here without Baba, just you and me and Hero!"

"Oh, for heaven's sake, Tara! Stop going on! Let's deal with one crisis at a time. You finish clearing up in here. I'd better start getting your father's things together. It's a good thing I got his winter coat back from the cleaners yesterday. He'll need it up in the mountains. It's still very cold at night up there at this time of year."

6

Tara couldn't get to sleep that night. She had an awful feeling in the pit of her stomach. Every time she tried to think of comfortable, normal, everyday things a picture came into her mind of Baba, still feeling sick and shaky, running away in the night like some kind of criminal. She kept telling herself that people got through the mountain roads safely all the time. The pesh murgas were always sending people secretly in and out of town through the army lines from their mountain bases. But then she kept thinking of all the checkpoints on the roads. All it needed was one really alert soldier, one mistake from the people Baba was with. Not knowing whether he was safe or not was the worst thing.

She tossed and turned, and couldn't make herself comfortable. At last she rolled over and switched on the bedside light. She looked at her watch. It was well after midnight. And where was Granny? She usually went to bed quite early, but her bed was still empty. Tara sat up and swung her feet over onto her beautiful silk bedside rug. Ever since she'd been little, she'd always loved its intricate Persian patterns of leaves and flowers, and had never got up without wriggling her toes into its soft, cool pile. She did it now automatically. Its silky feel was comforting. Home was still home, even though Baba and Ashti had gone.

Tara opened the bedroom door. She could hear Granny and Daya arguing in the family sitting room. She shook her long hair back from her face, and went down the corridor. They didn't seem to notice her come into the room. Granny was sitting crosslegged on the carpet, her back stiff as a plank, her arms waving about as they always did when she had something on her mind. Tara sat down beside her.

"Don't be silly, Teriska. Of course you can't stay on here without Soran. There's no man in the house at all! It's out of the question. You've got to think about Tara. She's at a very sensitive age just now. You know perfectly well she's got to be properly looked after. You and I just can't do it. You know what it's been like since the war started. Dreadful things going on – do you know what Suzan said?"

Teriska Khan didn't want to know what Suzan said. She was sitting bolt upright too, and a red spot glowed in each cheek. She wasn't used to answering Granny back but she was obviously so upset she was past caring.

"You can't really be telling me that we've got to leave home, Mother! We couldn't possibly! Anyway, things are bound to get better soon. This business with Soran — it'll all blow over. It's got to! It did last time. He may be closely involved with the pesh murga leaders, but at least he's kept everything absolutely secret. Anyway, how do we know that man Mahmoud was telling the truth about those people coming today? He seemed a bit fishy to me. Why did he come here, and not phone up or something? I don't believe there's any real danger. Soran'll be home soon, and . . ."

"Is that what he told you?"

Teriska Khan shook her head reluctantly.

"No, but only this morning, Leila's mother, Mrs Amina was telling me . . ."

Granny snorted.

"Don't fool yourself, my girl. What does that woman know about anything? She's only half Kurdish herself! This war might go on for years. Anyway, what about Ashti? You've got to face facts. He's a deserter as far as they're concerned. If you don't join up once your papers have been sent that's what you are — a deserter. Ashti's committed a capital offence, and Kak Soran's committed a dozen at least, I shouldn't wonder. They'd be mad to show their faces in Sulaimaniya. Look what happened to your cousin Zhen's family! And those people we know in Mosul, the ones who ran that TV import business. Then there was . . ."

"Oh, don't! Stop it!" Teriska Khan put her fingers in her ears. "Don't tell me any more awful stories, Mother. I can't bear it."

"Do you mean," said Tara, "that Baba and

Ashti won't ever come back? Ever?"

"They will, of course they will," said Teriska Khan, groping for a tissue.

"No, they won't," said Granny firmly. "They can't. Not until this war's over and we get a new government, anyway. You should leave here at once, Teriska, and join them."

Teriska Khan blew her nose.

"Leave? Leave home?" said Tara. "How long for?" She felt bewildered.

Granny patted her knee.

"Don't ask me, dear. I wish I knew when this war will end. So does everyone else."

Teriska Khan's eyes were wandering round her lovely sitting room. Granny saw, and jabbed a finger at her.

"I didn't bring you up to cling to luxury while your husband and son struggle along without home comforts in the mountains!" she said accusingly. "The family's always got to come first, before carpets, and sofas, and goodness knows what else. Whatever happens, you must stick together."

"You know perfectly well, Daya," interrupted Teriska Khan furiously, "that the family means more to me than anything else in the world. But we can't just pack up and go! There's a whole lot of business to see to. The house, the car . . . And Tara's got her exams coming up very soon now, and Hero's only just started in kindergarten. Their education . . ."

Granny sniffed.

"You know my views on education," she said crushingly. "It does nothing but fill girls' heads with irreligious nonsense, and turn them against their homes and their husbands. Let them study the Koran. That's all the book learning they need. When I was a girl . . ."

Tara and Teriska Khan exchanged looks. They'd heard this conversation a dozen times before. Tara knew that the well-worn arguments would go backwards and forwards for another half hour at least.

"Granny," she said, as soon as Granny paused for breath, "do you really think we've got to go away?"

"Now listen, my dear," said Granny, taking one of Tara's hands in hers and patting it gently. "You're a big girl now. Almost grown up. I was getting my wedding clothes together when I was your age. You've got to understand that it's all for your own safety. What your mother doesn't seem to grasp is that it's just plain dangerous for you all to stay here. It's not only the pesh murgas who are wanted men. It's like I always say, "Sit near the forge and you'll get sparks in your face." Whole families of the pesh murgas are arrested sometimes. And I don't have to tell you that women prisoners are not treated with respect. Why, the stories I've heard . . ."

Tara shuddered. Granny had told her some of them only yesterday.

"But I need time," said Teriska Khan desperately. "I can't just walk out, like that. I've got to pack everything, to get hold of some money. I mean there's hundreds of things . . ."

"Pack?" Granny sounded scornful. "You can't take all this with you." She swept out an arm, as if she was dismissing all the rugs and cushions, the little tables with their lamps and ornaments, the tapestries on the walls and the TV set and video in their own special cabinet. "You can take as much as you can load into one taxi, and you shouldn't bother yourself with anything except some warm clothes, a few cooking things and medicines. Oh, and blankets of course. By the way, Teriska, did you do what I told you with your jewellery?"

The fight seemed to have gone out of Teriska Khan. She nodded.

"If you'll take my advice," said Granny firmly, "you'll leave as soon as possible. Tomorrow."

"Aren't you coming with us, Granny?" said Tara anxiously. Granny might be very strict sometimes, and she didn't understand about school, but she was so wise and solid, such a rock, on which you felt you could lean, that Tara felt an awful sense of panic at the idea of leaving her.

"I'm going back to Suzan in Baghdad, dear," said Granny, "once I've made sure you've all got off safely. The mountains are no place for an old woman like me. I'd only get in the way and hold you all up. Anyway, Suzan needs me. Now take that anxious look off your face and help me get up. It's time we were all in bed. No one's going to come for you tonight, Tara, so we can all go and get some sleep."

It was hard to see how Granny could know, but she sounded so certain that Tara just obeyed her, and got back into bed, and fell asleep at once, and it wasn't until she woke up the next morning that she realized she had probably slept in her own bed in her old home for the very last time.

7

The next day was Friday, the one day of the week when schools and offices were closed. Granny refused to break her normal routine. She went off into Sulaimaniya to the mosque. Even though she never usually missed Friday prayers, and spent several hours in the women's gallery every week, Tara somehow hadn't expected her to go this time.

"I didn't think there'd be time today," she said, feeling a bit let down as Granny put on her black veil over her dress and got ready for the taxi that Tara had called for her.

"We need all the prayers we can get right now," said Granny. She put her arms round Tara and gave her an extra tight hug. Tara felt the old arms trembling and looked up into Granny's puckered face.

"You're a good girl," said Granny. She seemed about to say something else, but the taxi driver rang the doorbell and she thought better of it.

When Tara shut the door behind Granny the house felt strangely empty. Teriska Khan, who'd got up in the small hours and had been frantically packing things away in cupboards and cleaning and defrosting the cooker and fridge, had gone out to see her cousin, a lawyer.

"Lucky for us your father had almost sold the car before he left," she said to Tara. "I've only got to hand over the papers and we'll have the money in our pockets."

Tara hated the idea that she'd gone for her last ride in the big, comfortable Mercedes, but there was no time to brood about it.

"Get your things ready while I'm out," Teriska Khan said before she left. "I've packed most of your clothes already, but you can take one small bag of your own things. Now do be sensible, darling. The village isn't the place for silly shoes, and there's no electricity so don't bother with your hairdryer, or records, or anything like that. We'll leave sometime this afternoon, if we can. You'll be all right while I'm out. I'm sure they won't come on a Friday. And look after Hero."

Tara went to the bedroom and looked about despairingly. How could she possibly pack all her favourite things into one small bag? She looked into the cupboard, and touched the strap of the lovely handbag Granny had given her only last year. Then she saw an old fluffy toy she'd had since she was a baby. She looked up at the poster of Najleh Fathee, her favourite actress, that smiled down at her from the wall. What was the point in taking any of them?

Quickly she opened her drawers and got out her jewellery, a couple of lovely silk scarves Leila had given her, and a make-up set she'd bought in Sulaimaniya a few weeks ago. Then she ran her finger along the backs of her schoolbooks. She'd leave 'English made Easy' behind without any regrets at all, but she could hardly bear to look at the others. A few weeks ago, she'd wished like anything she wasn't in the middle of exams. She'd thought she never wanted to sit another test again as long as she lived. But now that she really wasn't going to it all seemed quite different. She'd have given anything to have gone back to school with all the others tomorrow. The thought of no more homework, no more Maths, no more Mrs Avan, no more history, and science and geography made her feel confused, almost light headed. She couldn't imagine what she was going to do all day long.

"Tara! Tara!" Hero was calling.

"In here!" Tara shouted back.

She heard Hero's feet pattering down the corridor, then saw her face appear round the door.

"What do you want?" said Tara. The last thing she wanted was Hero pulling her things round at the moment.

"I want . . ." Hero said vaguely, not knowing how to answer.

"Well, go and play with something," said Tara, turning her back.

"I want a biscuit!" said Hero triumphantly. "I want a biscuit, want a . . ."

"Oh, all *right*," said Tara. "I'll get you one."

She followed Hero out of the room and down the corridor to the kitchen. She was opening the food cupboard when the door bell rang.

"There's a man there," said Hero.

"What? How do you know?"

"He was there before."

"Why didn't you tell me?"

"I wanted a biscuit. You never said about the man."

"Quick," said Tara, grabbing a packet of biscuits and shoving it into Hero's hand. "Go and watch your cartoon video."

The doorbell rang again.

"Hurry up!" said Tara desperately, giving Hero a little push. "Bugs Bunny and Donald Duck."

She shut the family sitting room door and hurried towards the front door. Daya had said they wouldn't come on a Friday. It might just be somebody ordinary. She tried to peer through the frosted glass panel in the front door. There were two tall dark shapes standing outside.

"Who's there?" she called.

A strange man's voice answered.

"Open up. I wish to speak to Mr Soran."

"He's not here," said Tara. Her heart had begun to thump uncomfortably hard. This didn't sound like a friend or a neighbour.

"Where's Mr Soran?"

Tara found she could think wonderfully clearly and quickly. She remembered every word that Mr Mahmoud from Baba's office had said.

"He's in Baghdad," she said, making her voice sound as normal as she possibly could.

She heard the two men talking together in low voices.

"Why hasn't he taken his car?"

"They've been snooping round the back," thought Tara. She could hear music coming from the sitting room. Hero's cartoon was starting.

"Stay in there, please Hero," she thought urgently. Aloud she said,

"He's getting a new car. He's gone to Baghdad to fetch it. He's sold our old one."

The men didn't seem to hear.

"Open the door!" one said roughly. "We'll wait for him inside."

"I — I can't," said Tara, hoping she could still keep one jump ahead. "My mother's taken the keys of the house with her."

"Where's your mother? Why isn't she at home?"

"She's gone into town."

"What's her business in town?"

"I don't know. I think — I think she's handing over the papers to the lawyer, something to do with the car."

She jumped back with a shock as one of the men loudly rattled on the door handle, trying to open it.

"Locked," she heard him grunt. "The kid's telling the truth. The woman was seen going into the lawyer's house. Nothing we can do now but wait."

Tara watched their fuzzy shapes retreat out of the garden gate. She ran to a window and peeped out. A long sleek grey car was pulled up at the end of the road, under the shade of a tree. The two men walked down the road to it, and got in. Tara watched and waited but it didn't drive away.

The next half an hour until her mother came home seemed to last a century. Luckily, Teriska Khan came in the back way, out of sight of the waiting car. She went pale when Tara pointed it out to her. Together, they peered through the net curtains at it. It was a few hundred yards away, but they could clearly see a third man handing something into it from the outside. It looked like a tray of food.

"That's it then," said Teriska Khan. "My mother was right. I was an idiot not to leave yesterday. Go next door, Tara, and ask Mrs Amina if we can leave from the back entrance to Haji Feisal's house. She knows we're going today. She promised to do anything she could for us, and to look after the house and keep the keys until we — if ever — " she didn't finish her sentence.

"But they'll see me," said Tara.

"Go over the garden wall, at that place where the oleander comes right down low, like you used to when you and Leila were little," said Teriska Khan. "Ask Leila to run out and find a taxi to come to the back gate, then come back and help me with the bags. Are they moving yet? No, look, they're eating. Hurry up, Tara. And take Hero with you."

Tara felt as if every nerve in her body was tingling. She had never been so alive before. She ran into the sitting room. A new cartoon was just starting. Tara snapped the TV off. Hero let out a wail.

"Please, not now," begged Tara. "No tantrums just now. You've just got to do what I say."

Hero looked up at her and kicked her feet defiantly. Tara made her voice sound as bright and enticing as she could.

"I've got a treat for you."

Hero stopped kicking.

"We're going next door to see Auntie Amina. Leila'll give you a cake, I expect."

"Leila!" Hero jumped up, pleased.

"And we're going to climb over the wall.

"No, no! Not the wall! The gate!"

"It's all right Hero, the dog's chained up. He won't bite you. Come on! Hurry!"

Hero ran ahead to the back door, but then she darted round Tara and back to the sitting room again.

"My rabbit!" she said.

"There's no time for that! Quick!" Tara's voice dropped its coaxing tone. She was starting to feel panicky. She tried to catch Hero, but missed, and Hero dodged round and snatched up her blue floppy eared rabbit from where she'd thrown it down on the sitting room cushions.

Tara bundled her out of the house, skirted round the wall of the garden to the shade of the oleander tree and lifted her up.

Mrs Amina, Leila's mother, was standing at her kitchen door. She took in the situation at once, took Hero out of Tara's arms, and gave her a hand over the wall.

"We need a taxi right now!" panted Tara. "They're down at the end of the street in a car. They're eating, but they might be here any minute."

Leila came out of the house too.

"You'll never get a taxi at this time of day," she said.

Tara dropped Hero's hand. All her clear-headedness had drained away. She couldn't think any more.

"What'll we do?" she wailed.

"Where's your mother?" said Mrs Amina.

"She's getting the bags, locking up – I don't know."

Mrs Amina ran to her kitchen window.

"Quick, Tara, the car's moving. It's coming down the road. Call your mother to leave the bags and get over here at once. I'll get your stuff to you later if I can. I'll drive you myself. Quick!"

Tara raced back to the wall. Teriska Khan was at the back door, fussing over a bag. Tara called to catch her attention. Teriska Khan looked up. Tara mimed the men in the car, coming down the road. Teriska Khan pulled the door shut behind her, turned the key, picked up the two biggest bags and raced to the oleander tree. Then she ran back for the others.

"Leave them! Leave them, Daya!" hissed Tara.

"They'll get you!"

As Teriska Khan reached the shade of the oleander, she started at the sound of a car door slamming outside the front gate of the house. Tara leaned over, took the bags from her one by one, and lifted them over the wall. Her hands were so sweaty she nearly couldn't hold onto the handles.

"Leave them, Daya, never mind the bags! Just climb!" she whispered.

"Can't," panted Teriska Khan. "If we leave them here they'll know Mrs Amina helped us. There's the samovar. I can't leave that behind! Take my hand, Tara, quick!"

She scrambled over the wall and dropped down panting on the other side. Mrs Amina had already run to the car with the first load of bags. Tara and Leila raced to the carport with the others. Teriska Khan scooped up Hero, and jumped into the car.

Luckily, Leila's father, Haji Feisal usually parked his car round the back of the house, and drove it out into a side street, which was out of sight of the road at the front of Kak Soran's house. Mrs Amina jumped into the driver's seat, switched on the engine, and clashed into first gear. The car jerked forwards and the passengers were flung backwards, as the car bolted out into the street.

"Goodbye, Leila," Tara mouthed through the window, but she only had time to catch a last glimpse of Leila as the car gathered speed. She craned her neck round but all she could see was the white garden wall of her old home, the pretty round arch over the gateway smothered with clusters of scarlet bougainvillea, dazzlingly bright in the strong sunlight.

"I didn't know you could drive," said Teriska Khan, shutting her eyes as Mrs Amina swerved round the corner so wide she nearly knocked over the old fruit seller, who was squatting as usual by the side of the road.

"I've had four lessons so far," said Mrs Amina through clenched teeth.

"Daya! What about Granny?" said Tara suddenly.

"She's going on to Uncle Dilshad's after Friday prayer," said Teriska Khan. "She said she'd phone before she tried to come back to the house. She thought we might have to go in a hurry."

"But I didn't say goodbye to her!" said Tara miserably.

Teriska Khan didn't answer. She was too busy clutching at the side of her seat as Mrs Amina swung across the road to avoid a truck, which was bearing down on them, hooting fiercely.

"Can you drop us at the bus station?" she said faintly. "We'll get a taxi there."

"Yes, of course," said Mrs Amina, turning to look at Teriska Khan for so long that Teriska Khan had to restrain herself from grabbing hold of the steering wheel.

"Now, don't look so worried, my dear. I'll keep an eye on the house and everything for you. It'll all be safe with me."

8

It was three or four years since Tara had come to the mountains, and she'd never been there in the springtime before. They'd often come before the war, when she was little. In the summer holidays, when it got so blisteringly hot in Sulaimaniya that the tarmac melted on the road, Kak Soran would pile the whole of his family into the car and drive them up to the old house he still owned in the village, where his grandfather had been born.

Tara loved these holidays. She was vaguely related to half the village children, and they all used to play together. They'd spent hours squatting on the ground, making wonderful walls and ditches in the mud, and they'd scrambled around and outside the village wherever they liked, through the close-packed lanes, in and out of each other's houses which were stacked up in tiers against the hillside, and over the rough, rocky terrain outside keeping an eye open for scorpions.

Mrs Amina dropped them on the edge of Sulaimaniya, quickly said goodbye, and jumped back into the driving seat with understandable relief.

Teriska Khan coughed to clear the lump in her throat.

"I never thought she was so fond of us," she said, closing her eyes to avoid witnessing Mrs Amina being crushed to death in what seemed like an inevitable collision with a bus. "She's taken an awful risk." She opened her eyes. Mrs Amina had miraculously scraped past the bus and was disappearing down the road in a burst of exhaust fumes.

"So did we when we got into her car," said Tara. "Did you see the way she took that last corner?"

"Don't be ungrateful, darling," said Teriska Khan, signalling to a hovering taxi driver. "She probably saved our lives."

The journey took hours and hours but Tara enjoyed it all the same. She kept remembering things. That was the bend in the road where they'd once had a puncture. It had taken ages to fix. And over there they often used to stop for a picnic. She and Ashti had found a couple of baby tortoises once, just beyond those rocks.

But at the same time, as the taxi ground its way up and round the tortuous winding road, she knew in the back of her mind that something awful was happening. They were leaving home. They might never be able to go back again. She might have seen Leila, and all her friends for the last time. The problem was, she couldn't really believe it. The taxi and the road and Daya and

Hero all seemed too ordinary, too familiar.

In one way though it wasn't familiar. The countryside looked much nicer in the spring than in the summer, when she was used to seeing it. The high peaks were still white with snow, but the fields on the lower slopes, which by July were always bare and brown and dusty, were covered with fresh green growth at this time of year. In the valleys, the streams were full of clear clean water, and there were orchards of almond and apricot trees covered with beautiful clouds of blossom. When they passed a flock of sheep, herded by a couple of elderly turbaned Kurds, Tara could see dozens of leggy, woolly lambs.

"This is it, what it's all about. Kurdistan," she thought. She'd only been a kid when she'd been here before. She'd never even noticed how beautiful it all was.

"Would I die for Kurdistan, like that boy?" she thought, and shivered.

"Look at that blossom, Daya," she said, to break the silence.

Teriska Khan only grunted. She was hugging her samovar, too anxious to talk, in case they might be held up at a police checkpoint, and by the time she'd looked in the direction of the blossom, she couldn't have seen much anyway through the dancing fringe of blue pompoms that the taxi driver had fixed above the windscreen.

It was lovely arriving at the old village house, almost like the first night of a childhood holiday. They got there just as the sun was disappearing below a high snow-capped peak. The road didn't go up as far as the village and they had to walk the last few hundred yards to the closely packed, flat-roofed houses which clung to the steep hillside. They were standing where the taxi had dropped them, wondering how they could carry all their bags and bundles, when Hero suddenly yelled,

"Baba! It's my Baba!"

Tara looked up. A man was running down the hillside to meet them. It took Tara a moment to recognise him. He was wearing baggy striped trousers, a huge cummerbund and a loose-sleeved shirt, and had a turban tied round his head. It was Kak Soran all right but he looked younger and fitter than he did in his usual western style suit.

"Oh, thank God," said Teriska Khan. She sat down on a suitcase for a moment, and Tara thought she must be feeling funny, but a minute later she got up, took a bundle in one arm and a bag in the other, and started up the winding path.

Tara went after her, sniffing the air. She'd forgotten this lovely fresh mountain smell, mixed with a homely whiff of woodsmoke from the evening fires on which everyone's suppers were being cooked.

She'd forgotten the sounds of the mountains too. The air was so clear you could hear the smallest noise for miles. Even from this distance she could hear people talking and laughing in their houses in the village, and the clinking of pots and pans. At home, sounds like that were buried under a general sludgy noise of traffic, and machinery, and the humming of things like air-conditioning. Here, the only mechanical sound was the drone of the taxi, disappearing into the distance.

Hero was running ahead up the rough stony path, holding her rabbit by one leg, but she suddenly stopped and screeched with fright. A huge white bird with long red dangling legs was flapping over her head. Tara laughed.

"It's a stork," she said. "Look, he's got a nest on that roof over there."

The stork landed awkwardly on its nest, settled itself down, then laid its neck along its back, lifted up its long beak and clacked it open and shut with a deafening clatter. Hero grabbed hold of Tara's leg and clung to it as if she was a baby monkey.

"He's only old Haji Laqlaq," said Tara impatiently, taking her hand and pulling her along. "He's a Haji because he flies off to Mecca every summer, and Laqlaq because of the noise he makes. Come on, don't be silly! Look, Baba's waiting for you!"

Tara had always loved night time in the village house. There wasn't a separate bedroom. At bedtime they had to drag out the thick quilts and solidly stuffed pillows that were piled up against the wall and lay them out on the beaten earth floor. The whole family slept together, lying in a row.

Tara used to lie looking up at the bare wooden rafters that supported the roof, and count the knots in the gnarled old wood till Baba put the oil lamp out, and then usually the fresh mountain air, and the way she'd been running about all day made her so sleepy, that she'd turn her head over on the bright print pillow and fall asleep at once.

But tonight she lay awake for a long time, listening to the sounds outside. An owl hooted in the old walnut tree outside the courtyard. A dog barked at the other end of the village. Somewhere, miles up the cold air, an aeroplane was buzzing.

It wasn't the sounds that were keeping her awake though. She couldn't get out of her mind the sight of Leila, standing at the gate where they'd always met on the way to school. Then, when Leila faded, all she could see was the scarlet bougainvillea against the white garden wall, with the sun blazing on it. The sinister grey car and the two shadowy men were lurking somewhere at the edge of her mind, but they seemed to belong to a dream world, or a film she'd once seen long ago. She could hardly believe all that had happened.

"I wish I'd said goodbye to Granny properly," she thought, and a few minutes later, "I wish I'd packed my new red sweater." Then she was asleep.

She didn't wake up until quite late. Kak Soran was coughing. He still hadn't really got over his virus. Teriska Khan was up and dressed already, and fumbling through one of the bags.

"You're awake, are you?" she said to Tara. "You'd better give me what you were wearing yesterday to pack away. You can't wear town clothes here. Put these on."

She tossed over a pair of long loose trousers, a light green, long-sleeved underdress, and an overdress in a bright shimmering material.

Tara stood up, yawned, stretched and began to get dressed in her Kurdish clothes, modestly wriggling into her trousers and underdress before she took her nightdress right off.

It was still almost dark in the room. There were heavy wooden shutters over the windows which blocked out most of the early morning light. As Tara groped about, feeling for the fringed scarf she was supposed to wear over her hair, her fingers touched a belt. She picked it up. It was extraordinarily heavy.

"What on earth's this, Daya?"

Teriska Khan almost snatched it out of her hand.

"Just my old belt. Why?"

"It feels so heavy."

"Nonsense."

Teriska Khan put the belt round her own waist, and did up the buckle. Then she stepped over Hero, who was still fast asleep, and went to the door, which led directly out onto the courtyard. She unbolted and opened it. Sunlight streamed into the room. Hero mumbled something, then rolled over, reached out for her rabbit, and went on sleeping.

Tara could see now what Daya was wearing. She looked completely different from the smart western style woman she was at home, where she usually wore elegant designer dresses and well-cut suits. If her skin had been all weatherbeaten instead of properly moisturised, and her hands had been chapped and calloused with rough work instead of nicely manicured, she could almost, at first sight, have been taken for a woman of the village.

Her long underdress was made of bright scarlet cotton, with a pattern of gaudy flowers printed on it. The bodice was tight, but the gathered skirt was full. The sleeves were slit half way down to allow her hands out, and they were so long that they would have trailed on the ground if they hadn't been tied together with a knot behind her back. On top she wore a flimsy, gauzy overdress, which did up with a single button at the waist so that the skirt and bodice of the underdress peeped through. The finishing touch was a scarf which she was putting round her head and tying at the back. It had a pretty fringe which dangled over her eyes.

"Kurdish clothes are great," Tara thought. "Much nicer than all those boring old city clothes." The funny thing was that you could spend a fortune on just one dress imported from London or Paris, and look really dull, while Kurdish country women, who never had a penny to spare, dressed in lovely bright colours and shiny materials and looked like princesses every day of the week.

The small square room had been closed up all

night, and it had been really stuffy with the four of them sleeping in it. Tara went outside, slipped her feet into her shoes which she'd left at the door, and almost gasped as the cold air of a spring morning hit her face. She looked over at the peaks of the high Zagros that soared up on the far side of the valley into the few fluffy clouds, still tipped with dawn pink. On the other side of those mountains was Iran. She'd always wondered what it was like over there.

"Hello," said a voice behind her. Tara turned round. A girl was coming out of the second house in the compound, with a baby perched on her hip.

"Are you Kak Soran's daughter?" she said shyly.

Tara thought for a moment, then she smiled.

"Ghazal!" she said. She remembered this girl, a distant cousin Daya had said, from visits years ago. She'd never imagined that Ghazal would be married already, and with a baby too. It seemed only a couple of years ago that they'd been playing houses together. She went up and tickled the baby's feet.

"He's sweet," she said admiringly. "How old is he? What's his name?"

"His name's Naman," said Ghazal proudly. "He's just six months."

"Ghazal!" a hoarse, bossy voice called from the kitchen at the back of the house.

"My mother-in-law wants her breakfast," said Ghazal, pulling a face. "Are you staying for long?"

"I don't know," said Tara. "Yes, I suppose so." She wished Ghazal hadn't asked. It wasn't something she wanted to think about. She wanted to pretend for a bit longer that she was only there on holiday, like in the old days. It was fun doing without electric lights and cooking over a fire, and fetching water from the spring for a week or two. She wouldn't even try to imagine what it would be like living here for ever, never having a proper bath again, never watching TV, or sitting in a comfortable armchair. She'd end up like Ghazal, married to a man who was away from home most of the time, and having to obey her mother-in-law.

She watched Ghazal go, then heard Teriska Khan clattering around in the dark little kitchen that was no more than a lean-to tacked on to the rear wall of the house. She came out with a water pot in her hand.

"Run up to the spring, Tara, and fill this," she said. "I'll get the fire going. It'll take hours for the samovar to heat up."

Tara remembered the spring. It bubbled out of a mossy crack in the rock above the village, and cascaded down a well-worn channel to the pool several hundred yards below. The pool was a lovely place, with willows and oleander trees all round it. The village women always met there. It was the only place where you could wash yourself and your clothes and properly clean pots and pans. In the summer it was lovely at the pool, when the water felt cool and refreshing, but Tara shivered at the idea of washing in it at this time of year.

She picked up the water pot and set off up the stony path. "I suppose Leila will be going to school by herself around now," she thought. "I wonder if she's thinking of me?"

There was a sudden awful screech above her head. A jay was perched in the old walnut tree, whose branches hung down low across the path. He was scolding her angrily.

He looked so indignant that Tara laughed. He bobbed his head, and with a flash of his brilliantly coloured wings, he soared away across the hillside and settled in a blossom-laden apricot tree.

Tara turned to watch him go, and then she gasped. She'd never seen anything so beautiful in her life before. The earth on that part of the hillside, which she'd only ever seen when it was baked hard and brown in the hot summer months, was now a patchwork of brilliant colours. Through the shoots of fresh green grass, a vast carpet of spring flowers shimmered in the breeze, as rich as the silk Persian rug in which she used to wriggle her feet into at home. Clumps of wild scarlet tulips and white narcissus stood highest, and in between were violets and anenomes. Budding spikes showed where, in a month or two, hollyhocks and teazels would burst into flower.

Tara felt suddenly full of energy. Kurdistan! she thought. This is Kurdistan! and she bounded up the last steep stretch of path to the spring. It had always been a favourite place of hers.

Just below the place where it gushed out of the rock, where the woman came to fetch their drinking water, the villagers had built what they called a *gazino*, a sort of comfortable summerhouse. They'd cut some strong branches and laid them over the stream a few yards below the spring, and built a rather rough and ready roof of leafy branches overhead. On a boiling summer's day, it was a heavenly place to sit after a hot climb. The cold water running beneath it kept it beautifully cool.

Tara could see the gazino now, just above her head. She looked at it, trying to remember. Surely it hadn't been quite like this? The walls hadn't been so thick, she was sure, and there'd only been a light screen of twigs and leaves through which the slightest breeze could filter. She came up level with it. On this side there'd been a low entrance. You'd had to bend your head to get inside. Now there was a heavy wall of sandbags, completely blocking a view of the inside.

Tara was about to stand on tiptoe to peer in when she heard low voices and movements coming from behind the sandbag wall. She stepped back, trying not to make the loose stones on the path rattle under her feet, and hurried on up the last ten yards to the spring. Whoever was using the gazino now, they obviously weren't ordinary village people. Nobody would be resting and chatting at this time of day. Everyone was hard at work.

Tara filled her pot, tiptoed back past the sandbags and hurried down the rest of the path home. Kak Soran met her half way down.

"Your mother told me you'd gone for water," he said. "I came up to warn you. There's a pesh murga lookout up there, guarding the spring. They won't do anything to you, but don't talk to them or take any notice of them if you have to go up there again."

"All right, Baba," said Tara. She followed him back down the path. She wasn't very used to being with him on her own. She wanted to point out the flowers, and talk about Kurdistan, only she felt too embarrassed. But when they got to the place where she'd stopped to watch the jay earlier, he stopped too, and turned round.

"Listen to this," he said.
"I am a wild rose, a rose of the mountains,
   Far, far away.
   O careful gardener, who loves the rose,
   Come and pick me.
   Carry me over the mountain.
   If you do not touch me
   I shall not flower.
   If you do not touch me
   I shall shed no fragrance."

She'd never heard him recite poetry before. She was so happy she felt six inches taller, and light on her feet.

"I was thinking too," she said, "about that

story in the Koran where Satan comes to the Prophet Adam in Paradise, and he makes him eat the fruit from the tree."

Kak Soran looked amused.

"I have got a well educated daughter," he said.

"Well," said Tara shyly, "it's just that the flowers and the nice old gazino up by the spring made me think of Paradise, but the war, and being frightened, and the guns – they're sort of like Satan coming into Paradise."

She was afraid he was going to laugh, but he didn't.

"I know exactly what you mean," he said, and they walked back down into the village together.

9

At first Tara felt safe in the mountains. She might hate having nothing to do all day, and she missed school and Leila with an awful kind of ache, but at least there were no watchers in sinister cars and no danger that the secret police would suddenly knock on the door and take Baba away.

The mountains were a no-go area as far as the government, the army and the police were concerned. The pesh murgas were in control.

But it didn't take long for that comfortable safe feeling to go. You couldn't spend much time in the village without noticing that everyone was waiting for some kind of showdown. You couldn't help noticing the ruins either, some inside and some outside the village, where bombs and shells from the last battle between the government troops and the pesh murgas had ripped gaping holes in walls and roofs and blasted out deep craters in the ground.

Down at the washing pool the village women all had a different opinion about when and where the next big action would be, and how it would turn out.

The optimists had a cheerful faith in their mountains and their fighters. Kurdistan was a natural fortress. The Kurds had always seen off armies from the plains through thousands of years of history. As they soaped and scrubbed and rubbed at their mounds of dirty washing the women swopped stories of the daring of the pesh murgas, who could appear from nowhere, carry out a raid or an ambush and melt away as if by magic up the rough mountainsides they knew so well.

The pessimists didn't say much. They didn't have to. They just pointed at the sky. There wasn't a lot that even pesh murgas could do against jet fighters and bombs.

Ghazal's mother-in-law, Baji Rezan, was the most talkative of them all. She always had the latest news with all the details. She was down at the washing pool when Tara and Teriska Khan took down their first week's load of laundry the morning after they'd heard the screams of low flying jets and the crump of distant explosions some way off to the north.

"Baji Rezan'll know all about it, you wait and see," whispered Teriska Khan as she and Tara came out through the screen of willows and joined the group of women at the edge of the pool. She was right.

"Over on the other side, it was," Baji Rezan was saying, pointing with her chin across the valley. She had big muscular arms and they bulged as she wrung out a course cotton sheet between her strong hands. "Three planes, and they came in so low you'd have thought they'd scrape the rooftops. The mosque was hit, and several houses. My brother-in-law was over that way yesterday. He didn't say how many people were killed but it must have been a good many. I know Hesho Khan's daughter was badly hurt."

"You don't think they'll come here next do you?" said Tara anxiously to Ghazal, who was scrubbing away at a pile of grubby baby clothes.

"That's what we'd all like to know!" Baji Rezan overheard and answered for her. She was squatting down, working at a stain on a dress.

She looked up at Teriska Khan and smiled, showing two gold teeth in the front of her mouth. "Can't you tell us? Your husband's supposed to have contacts everywhere. He must be in the know."

A look that Tara knew very well crossed Teriska Khan's face. It meant she didn't like the question and wasn't going to answer it. She had learned to be as discreet about Kak Soran's political activities as he was himself.

"He never talks about things like that to me," she said, sounding rather prim. Baji Rezan tossed her head, and looked round the circle of women.

"No need to be stand-offish," she said touchily. "We're not like your smart ladies in Sulaimaniya."

Teriska Khan smiled, to show she wasn't offended, and picked up another shirt. Baji Rezan seemed to feel she'd gone too far.

"Don't mind me," she said with a raucous laugh. "Everyone knows me. I always speak my mind. Take no notice of me." She dug Tara painfully in the ribs with her powerful elbow. Tara nearly toppled over into the pool. "When are you going to find a husband for this pretty girl, then? She must be nearly the right age. Got anyone in mind? Why don't you get Kak Soran to get on with it? It'd be nice to have a wedding in the village. Cheer us all up a bit. Take our minds off the war. Better choose the right night, though. My sister's daughter was married a few weeks ago, in a village up north. They chose that very night for a bombardment! The bride and groom had only had five minutes alone together when bombs started falling all round them. What a way to start your married life!"

The others all seemed to find this story funny, but Tara didn't. She blushed and felt embarrassed and miserable. She couldn't understand what she was doing here, washing clothes with people like this. None of these women were like her. None of them had been to a proper school, or travelled anywhere. Half of them had never even been out of the village, and only a few had been as far as Sulaimaniya.

They're so rough, she thought, and ignorant, and tactless. I can't spend the rest of my life with people like that! I can't!

After that, Tara tried not to go to the pool when all the other women were there. She didn't care how stuck up they thought her.

It wasn't hard to avoid them. Now that spring had well and truly come to the mountains, most of the women were hard at work in the fields in their vegetable patches, breaking their backs as they bent over their weeding and planting, and coming home exhausted to cook their husbands' dinners. Tara hadn't got much to do. Kak Soran didn't have any farm land of his own, and in any case, she told herself, she couldn't possibly have done farm labouring like the others.

She helped Daya, of course, but it didn't take long to finish her home chores, to fold up the beds and sweep the floor of the house in the morning, and help Teriska Khan with the cooking and clearing up. She didn't even have to look after Hero much. Hero was perfectly happy. She was out of doors all day, playing with two other little girls who lived nearby. They spent hours and hours chasing a little flock of newly hatched goslings round the courtyard, and pretending to cook and keep house in an old empty store room built against the courtyard wall.

The worst thing about living in the mountains was that it got so boring. Being bored was worse than being uncomfortable. Tara even stopped seeing the nice things after a while. She still went up to fetch water from the spring every morning but now she didn't bother to stop and look at the fields of wild flowers. She hardly even noticed when the tulips began to lose their scarlet petals.

She was noticing other things though. She

noticed that strings of visitors were coming to see Kak Soran, just like they used to in Sulaimaniya, only these men didn't wear smart suits and highly polished shoes, like the town visitors had. They came in baggy hand-woven trousers, belts stuffed with cartridges, and turbans bound round their heads. And when they came into the room (which Tara and Teriska Khan would quickly leave) they'd kick their shoes off at the door, put their rifles down on the floor, and sit cross-legged with their backs against the wall.

Tara never spoke to them, but she sometimes caught sight of their faces as she passed the open door when the lamp was lit after dark, and several times she thought she recognized someone. She was sure that some of these men, in the dress of pesh murgas, were the very same well-off businessmen who'd so often sipped coffee with Baba in his own guest sitting-room at home.

The visitors weren't the only mystery. Tara had spent a bit of time wandering about near the village, looking out for the old places she'd played in years ago. One day she went to look for a rock where she and some of the other little girls used to play jumping games. There was a tangle of brambles over it now, but under them, beside the rock, she could plainly see a pile of wooden boxes. She went back the next day to take another look but the boxes had gone.

A week later she almost ran into a string of mules, with dozens of curiously shaped crates and bundles loaded onto their backs, being driven up a little used track about half a mile away from the village. No one else was about. All the villagers were down in the fields further down the hillside. She slipped behind a clump of scrubby oak trees to watch without being seen. The two men driving the mules seemed to be unusually careful and nervous in case the mules slipped, or broke away from the path. They kept calling out warnings to each other in low voices, then one or other of them would dart forward to stop one of the mules' slim hooves stumbling on a stone, and they'd catch it by the strap round its head and steady it.

A day or two after she'd seen the mules, Tara was sitting in the courtyard trying to copy Teriska Khan, who was rolling up a tasty stuffing into vine leaves with flicks of her fingers. It looked easy but it wasn't.

"It's no good! Mine just don't come out right," Tara said in disgust, putting down a leaf that had torn itself in half.

"It's just a knack," Teriska Khan said. "Keep trying. You'll get it."

Tara was the first to hear the drone of an aeroplane overhead. She looked up, wondering where it was coming from, but before she could say anything, Teriska Khan had jumped up, spilling the vine leaves off her lap, and grabbed Hero, who was swinging on a low branch of the tree in the corner of the courtyard.

"Quick! Get inside!" she yelled to Tara,

running for the house. Tara jumped up, and tried to follow, but she still wasn't really used to her long flowing dress, and she tripped over her skirt and fell sprawling on the ground.

The plane roared overhead. Tara covered her head with her hands, and pressed herself into the dust. Seconds later the plane had gone and the sound began to die away. She looked up cautiously, half expecting another to hurtle past, but the sky was empty. Then she heard someone laughing behind her.

"What's the matter with you? Don't tell me you're scared! That was only a reconnaissance plane. The bombers come in much lower!"

"Ashti!" Tara scrambled to her feet. "What are you doing here? Where have you been all this time?"

Ashti had a rifle slung over his shoulder. He slipped it off and held it by its strap, so that it dangled carelessly from his hand.

Tara couldn't take her eyes off him. He looked completely different. For one thing he seemed to have grown at least a couple of inches since she'd last seen him. He was sunburnt. He looked sort of harder, and more muscular, and years and years older. She felt a bit shy of him.

"Military business, my dear," he said in a grand manner. He sounded like Uncle Rostam. "Not for the ears of little girls."

Even though he was her older brother and she was supposed to treat him with respect, Tara wasn't going to stand for that. She nearly said something indignant, but then she stopped herself. She knew a better way to deal with Ashti. She shrugged, and turned round as if she was about to walk off.

"Suit yourself," she said carelessly. "Don't tell me if you don't want to."

His sunburnt face cracked open into a grin, and he suddenly looked like the old Ashti again.

"Well, if you must know, we've ambushed an ammunition convoy. It was fantastic! You should have seen Rostam. He took the most incredible risks. There's no one like him. He's a hero!"

"You've captured a load of ammunition?" said Tara, feeling as though the pieces of a jigsaw were falling into place. "When?"

"Last week. Why?"

"Oh, nothing. I suppose they're hiding it somewhere?"

"Of course we are! But that's not for you to know about. No one's got any idea that we've got ammo stashed around here."

Tara smiled. Ashti had always been hopeless at keeping secrets. It was just like him to blurt it all out.

"Are you sure nobody knows?"

"Quite sure! And they'd better not find out! I shouldn't have said anything to you, even though you're only a girl. It's absolutely top secret. If you talk about it, I'll murder you. Even up here, there are government spies all over the place!"

"Well," said Tara, feeling pleased with herself at having got it all out of him, "I don't know about spies but there are vine leaves all over the place. I'd better pick them up and give them a good wash. We're supposed to be having stuffed vine leaves for lunch but when Daya sees you I expect she'll rush off and kill a chicken or something."

10

Summer, 1984

Spring turned into early summer so fast you could almost watch it happening. The blossom fell off the trees and each flower left behind a tiny green bubble that would soon start swelling up into a fruit. The water in the streams had been brimming up to the tops of their banks since the heavy winter rain, but now it was beginning to go down, and soon it would be back to its usual summer trickle. Haji Laqlaq, with a nestful of baby storks to feed, was hard at work from dawn to dusk, hunting for a constant supply of frogs and insects.

Time didn't seem to be passing very fast to Tara. She was lonely. She was beginning to feel sorry she'd been so hasty with Baji Rezan and the other village women. They'd got the message that she didn't want to be friendly and they were quite happy to ignore her in return.

Even Ghazal wasn't all that welcoming any more. She said "Hello" to Tara whenever she met her, but she didn't stop for a chat, and Tara, feeling left out, would be almost envious as she watched Ghazal go off to the washing pool with her friends, holding Naman balanced on her hip.

Tara would hear voices and bursts of laughter float up from behind the oleander trees and she'd wince, feeling sure they were talking about her and laughing at her.

She felt worst in the afternoons when the women didn't all go off to the fields. Sometimes they got together in one of their houses, usually Baji Rezan's, and she'd let them persuade her to tell them stories as they sat doing their sewing. Tara didn't feel welcome at these sessions, but she couldn't help overhearing some of what went on. Baji Rezan's voice was loud and rasping and it easily reached as far as Kak Soran's house, only a few yards away.

Baji Rezan always started with the traditional formula, which came out in a kind of singsong rhythm.

"When there was and there wasn't, there was nothing but God," she'd chant, and then she was off. Her stories were the good old-fashioned Kurdish ones about princesses and dragons, magic, and heroes and heroines falling in love. Tara could tell she told them brilliantly because the women never seemed to want to leave, and stayed as late as they could so that they had to rush through cooking the supper. Tara never heard more than tantalizing snatches, and she tried to persuade herself that she didn't care.

Ashti and Kak Soran kept coming and going

from the village. Sometimes they'd be away for days at a time. Sometimes they'd spend the evening talking with other men until late, and then roll themselves into their quilts to sleep with the rest of the family, but when Teriska Khan got up to open the shutters when it got light, Tara would see that they'd already gone.

Once, Rostam came. He made a terrific stir. The men all crowded round to talk to him. It was easy to see how much they admired him. The women wouldn't talk openly to him of course, but Tara knew, from the muffled gigglings and rustlings she could hear behind half-opened doors that most of them were having a good look. Rostam obviously enjoyed it all. He walked with a swagger, living up to his reputation as a fighter of fantastic daring.

The next day he'd gone. He just disappeared silently in the night. Tara couldn't help preening herself a little in front of Ghazal. She mightn't be very popular in the village, but at least she had a national hero for an uncle.

Even though everyone talked about the war all the time, life still had to go on as usual. It was the busiest time for the farmers. The vegetables were sprouting and had to be weeded and watered all the time. The summer wheat and barley had to be sown. There was quite a lot of damage caused by winter snows and frost to paths and irrigation channels and all that had to be repaired.

Every now and then there'd be a bit of real news, reports of a bombing, or a pesh murga raid on a garrison of government troops, or stories of a government informer, who'd been caught and shot. There were terrible accounts of whole towns turned to rubble and entire hillsides set on fire in government bombing raids. In spite of all the work that needed doing in the fields, the men would be away from home half the time, and the women would wait in agony to hear if they'd been wounded or killed.

No one bothered to keep worrying news away from Tara now. It would have been silly to try, anyway. Living more or less in one room as they were now, everyone always knew everything at once. It wasn't like the big house in Sulaimaniya, where Daya and Baba had been able to be on their own whenever they wanted to.

Tara could hardly take in the awful things everyone was talking about. The numbers of dead and the names of villages blown to pieces somehow didn't mean anything. It was like listening to the radio or watching the news on TV. It all seemed to be happening to other people, a long way away. And it was hard to believe that they were in immediate danger when things seemed so normal, and everyone was busy with their ordinary springtime work.

Perhaps that was why, when the bombers came, she was taken completely by surprise.

It was late in the afternoon. The sun was already going down behind the mountains. Where it still shone, it made all the colours look brilliant and intense, but the shadows were getting longer so fast you could almost see them moving. Tara had gone up to the spring for a pot of water, and she was coming down the hill on her way home again when she heard the roar of aircraft. She looked up. There were four of them, wicked black darts shooting across the golden sky. They were flying so low they had to gain height to skim over the tops of the hills. They were already out of sight when Tara heard two distant thuds, that echoed from hillside to hillside. She looked across the valley. A spurt of smoke with an orange flame in the middle was shooting up from a village on the other side.

Tara didn't hang around to see if the bombers had found their target. She ran down the hillside, water from her full pot spilling down her dress. Teriska Khan was already at the gate of the courtyard looking out for her, holding Hero by the hand.

"Quick!" she said. "We've got to get to the cave!"

"But they've gone," said Tara, putting her pot down.

"They'll be back," said Teriska Khan over her shoulder. "Follow me!" and she started running down the track that led around the shoulder of the hill to a small cave, which went back quite a long way into the rock.

They were only half way there when the roar came again. This time the planes weren't little black arrows on the far side of the valley but thundering, screaming pieces of machinery, hurtling directly overhead, and the falling bombs didn't land with a distant crump, but with shattering explosions that filled the air with suffocating smoke and deadly flying debris.

It was over so quickly that Tara hardly knew what had happened. When the first explosion came she felt something hit her on the back of the head. She was knocked over, and must have blacked out for a moment or two, but she opened her eyes almost at once, and tried to struggle back onto her feet. She could only just manage to sit up. Her legs seemed to have turned to water. People were rushing past her shouting to each other, pushing and shoving to get to the cave. Behind her, from the smoking village, she could hear injured people screaming. Daya and Hero had raced on. They were out of sight already. She had to follow them! She tried to stand up again, but she felt all muzzy and confused. Her legs just didn't seem to be working, and for a moment she thought she was going to faint.

Then she felt someone grabbing her arm and hauling her to her feet.

"Come on, love," said a rasping voice. It was Baji Rezan.

"It's — it's my head. I can't walk," whispered Tara.

Baji Rezan put her arm round her and half carried, half dragged her down the path. But they'd only managed to stagger a few yards when the terrifying roar came again. A single plane had got behind the main squadron. It skimmed over the nearest hilltop. The stream of people trying to run away were cruelly lit up by the very last rays of the sun. The pilot saw his chance and veered a little to drop his deadly load right on top of them. The plane was going so fast that most of the bombs went wide, but one landed a bit further down the path in front of Tara and Baji Rezan. All of a sudden there was nothing but a mass of dust and smoke hanging over the road where only a few seconds before there'd been a dozen or more people.

Tara shut her eyes and fell against Baji Rezan, who practically lifted her up. But a minute or two later, Baji Rezan skidded on the path. Tara looked down. What she saw made her stomach heave and she was nearly sick. The ground was spattered with blood. She'd nearly tripped over something. She forced herself to look at it once, quickly, then she turned her eyes away. It was an arm with a pulpy raw stump lying by itself right in front of them.

Tara felt everything start to go black again.

"You go on," she managed to say. "I can't move."

Baji Rezan didn't say anything. She just grunted, grabbed Tara round the waist and heaved her up and over her shoulder as if she'd been a sack of grain.

The blackness came and went for a few more minutes, then Baji Rezan put her down, and Tara found she could just about stand up in spite of the thundering pain in her head. She looked round.

They were outside the cave.

Tara had always thought that the cave was quite big. She'd been a little way into it before, but she'd never gone very far because she was afraid of snakes. Now she saw that it was actually quite small, much too small anyway to hold all the people who were trying to cram themselves into it.

Tara would never have thought there were so many people in the village. There seemed to be hundreds, all shouting and pushing and trying to force their way in. She saw Teriska Khan wildly gesticulating to a woman who was already in the cave, asking her in sign language to get Hero in. The woman seemed to understand, and reached over people's heads. Teriska Khan passed Hero in, and she disappeared into the crowd somewhere at the back of the cave.

Tara didn't even try to get herself in. There was no point. There'd be no room, and she hadn't got any strength left to push. Anyway, it didn't seem to matter any more. She couldn't seem to understand what was going on. She just wanted not to faint. She sat down and put her head down between her knees. Her whole skull and neck felt battered. She put her hand up and gingerly felt around. It came away sticky with blood. She turned her head cautiously, looking for Daya. She couldn't see her anywhere. There were too many scrambling, frantic people.

Suddenly, overhead, the dreadful screaming roar came again. The bombers were back. The people outside the cave flinched away from the noise, huddling uselessly together on the ground.

"I'm going to die," thought Tara. "I'm going to die now."

All around she heard people screaming. The sound wasn't even drowned out by the vicious roar of exploding bombs and the crackle and boom of what sounded like a million shells going off somewhere further down the hillside. After a while, she realized she was screaming herself.

She stopped all of a sudden because the breath was knocked out of her. Baji Rezan had thrown herself on top of her, spreading her arms and body out like a mother hen covering up a chick. Her sharp knee dug into Tara's thigh, and one of her buttons scratched Tara's cheek.

After what seemed like an hour but was actually less than a minute, Baji Rezan picked herself up.

"Come on, get up," she said, sounding incredibly calm. "They've gone. They won't come back today. They've got what they came for. Look."

She was pointing down the hillside. Tara looked. About half a mile away, a huge roaring fire was billowing up from the ground, explosions still shooting out from its centre. It was throwing rolls of flame and thick curls of choking black smoke up into the sky.

"There goes all the ammunition," said Baji Rezan. "I never thought they'd find it."

"Did you know about it?" said Tara, surprised.

"Yes, of course," said Baji Rezan. "What do you take me for?"

Tara suddenly wanted to cry. She flung her arms round Baji Rezan's sinewy neck and pressed her face into her shoulder. The sharp button scratched her again, but she didn't care.

"You saved me!" she said unsteadily.

Baji Rezan gave her a generous hug.

"You're a good girl," she said. "You'll do all right."

"You're like my Granny," Tara said, crying properly now. Baji Rezan stood up.

"I must find Ghazal," she said.

Tara tried to stop herself crying but found she couldn't so she just let the sobs come and the tears roll down her cheeks. She was still sitting on the ground. People were running around her in all directions, shouting and yelling. Babies were screaming. Injured people were groaning. Some were still inside the cave in case the bombers came back, but some were already racing down to the stream for water to put out the fires that were getting a hold on village houses. No one even bothered to think about trying to tackle the blazing ammunition dump. It was burning fiercely, and explosions were still going off in the middle of it. Its flames were lighting up the now almost dark hillside. The people scurrying up and down the path were silhouetted against its orange glare, and they looked like black insects.

Tara was still dizzy. She was only vaguely aware of the commotion going on all round.

"I'm alive," she said aloud.

She felt as if she'd made an astonishing discovery.

"I'm me," she thought. "I'm Tara. I'm the only person like me in the whole world."

11

That night Hero had her first bad dream. She screamed in her sleep and gave Tara such a fright that she bounced out of bed and was half into her clothes before she was properly awake.

No one tried to go back to sleep after that, even though it was at least an hour before dawn. Kak Soran had been working late the night before with all the other men to try to get the fire at the ammunition dump under control, and he'd gone to bed half dressed only about an hour earlier. He groped about in the dark for his warm felt waistcoat and went out to see how the fire-fighters were getting on.

Tara got dressed too, and went out after him, leaving Hero still crying in Teriska Khan's arms. She still had a bad headache, but she felt too restless to stay indoors. At least the dizziness of last night had gone. She wouldn't have been able to go round the village then. Even if she hadn't felt so battered, she couldn't have faced the idea of seeing anything worse than she'd seen already. She'd just felt relieved that their own house hadn't been turned into a pile of rubble, and all she'd wanted to do was lie down and be left alone.

There were twenty or thirty houses in the village. Six or seven had been completely destroyed, and most of the others seemed to be damaged. The worst of the fires had been put out and only a few smoking, glowing embers remained. Many of the courtyard walls that surrounded the village houses had gaping holes in them, and flickering oil lamps cast a lurid glow on the ruined buildings inside. The acrid smell of burning hung over the whole village and made Tara's eyes water.

The sky was getting lighter now and every minute she could see more clearly. Walls were cracked and bulging, doors had been blown out, bits of people's possesions were scattered everywhere. It was horrible to see private things, like a child's sweater or a woman's underclothes, lying on the public path, all torn and charred.

Most of the village seemed out and about, even though it was so early. Some people had obviously not been to bed all night. They'd either been trying to rescue some of their belongings from the wreckage, or they'd been looking after the injured. Others had been just too frightened to be inside. Now that it was getting light people were beginning to see which buildings were dangerously damaged, and they were trying to get their belongings out in case the roofs and walls collapsed.

Everyone looked shocked and emotional.

Those who weren't working were passing news of who'd been killed and who was injured, and discussing how soon the medical team would arrive.

Tara saw Baji Rezan stepping through a gaping hole in the wall round a neighbour's house. She clambered over a pile of fallen bricks to get to her.

"Are Ghazal and Naman all right?"

"Yes, thank God, they're fine. What about your parents?"

"They're all right."

"Thank God for that," said Baji Rezan again.

"Yes, thank God," repeated Tara. She'd often said those words before but she'd never really meant them like she meant them now.

The village seemed different after the bombing. It was as if they'd all been living in a fool's paradise. Lots of families had men with the pesh murgas, and for a long time there'd been news of casualties, and talk of bombings and battles in other places, but it had never come so close to home. The war had really reached them now.

It wasn't just the destruction. And it wasn't just the awful misery of the families of people who had died, though the sound of the crying and mourning was so sad that Tara could hardly bear to go out for a day or two. The real difference was the feeling of suspicion. No one said it out loud, but everyone was thinking the same thing. How had the government known where the ammunition dump was? Who had passed on the information? Which of their friends and neighbours was a spy?

Everything changed. There were no more story telling sessions in the afternoons in Baji Rezan's house. There wasn't much laughter or teasing at the washing pool either. Tara hadn't liked it at the time but she would have welcomed the teasing now. She felt she'd been silly and unfriendly before. She'd thought she was a cut above the village people. It was different now. She couldn't help admiring them. Even the ones who were bereaved or who'd lost their homes didn't complain much. They just picked up the next load of dirty clothes that needed washing, or the next basketful of vegetables that needed chopping up.

Tara still had a headache a lot of the time, and felt quite shaky, but people with worse things wrong with them were doing more than she was. When bombs started falling it didn't matter how good you were at Maths, or how rich your father was. The only important things were how brave you were, and how generous, and whether or not you could still have a good laugh.

Tara felt worst about the way she'd been rude to Baji Rezan. She'd never treated her with proper respect. But now, when Baji Rezan popped in for a visit, Tara jumped up and got her the best cushions, and ran out to the kitchen place round the back of the house to make tea. Before, she'd done as little as possible, and had left the entertaining to Teriska Khan. Baji Rezan didn't say anything, but her eyes twinkled, and she slapped Tara on the shoulder and chuckled with appreciation.

It wasn't long before the other village women started being more friendly too. Tara noticed it mainly at the washing pool. She didn't try to slip down there alone any more, but went with the others. They'd make room for her and advise her on how to wash her clothes. They could hardly believe that she'd never had to wash all her things by hand before, and they kept trying to get her to describe an electric washing machine and how it worked.

It wasn't really like being with her old friends of course. There was no one from her old life, who'd been to their home in Sulaimaniya or knew any of the families she'd been brought up with. No one understood about school, and how much she missed it, and how worried she was about getting left behind in her education.

There was just gossip about small, everyday things, like Naman's new tooth, and old Sara's obstinate cow that kept wandering off into the fields of new sprouting wheat and barley, and how strange old Nawa Khan had been since her grandson's body had been pulled out of the rubble of her house.

Tara still couldn't imagine staying in the village, planting cucumbers and looking after a flock of stupid hens and managing without electricity or a proper bathroom for ever more, but she was beginning to feel that in some ways the village was home.

Three weeks after the night of the

bombardment, Ashti came back. He was pale and thin, and he had his right arm in a sling. When she saw him, Teriska Khan jumped up from the pot she was stirring over the fire outside her little kitchen and hugged him. Then she turned away and wiped her eyes with the end of her long sleeve.

Tara thought, looking at them together, that Daya had lost weight too. It wasn't surprising. For one thing, no one had got much sleep since the bombing because Hero was still having nightmares every night. Tara was beginning to sleep through the racket she made, but Teriska Khan had to get up and comfort her until she dropped off to sleep again.

Tara went inside to get a stool, and put it in the shade of the apricot tree. It was getting too hot to sit outside in the sun now. Ashti sat down, and Teriska Khan squatted beside him.

"What happened? Are you badly hurt? Have you seen a doctor?"

Ashti looked embarrassed.

"Don't fuss, Mother. It's only my collar bone. There was a doctor up there and he set it. It's all right."

"But . . ."

"It's a clean break. He says it'll do fine, but I'm not to use it for a couple of weeks. I've got to keep my arm in a sling."

"How did it happen? Were you shot?"

Ashti shifted his weight on the stool, and pushed the hair out of his eyes with his good hand.

"It wasn't my fault! I couldn't help it. Rostam's so . . . Oh, I don't know. He just doesn't listen to you! I was doing what he told me, bringing up the ammunition even though we were in a really exposed position and getting shot at all the time, but the boxes were so heavy! They weighed a ton! I had to put mine down for a second, but there was no need for Rostam to yell at me in front of all the others, that I was scared and lazy and all the rest of it. He as good as said I wasn't pulling my weight, and was letting the rest of them do all the dangerous work.

"We were in a dug out kind of place, and it was the usual kind of ambush, but this time they were ready for us, must have had a tip-off or something, and they fought like tigers. We weren't expecting it at all. We used up all our mortars, and I was bringing up more, like I told you. Well, I'd put my box down, and Rostam saw me and yelled at me like a madman, so I was bending over to pick it up again when one of their mortars fell right near me. I didn't just lie down in a panic like Rostam said! It knocked me off my feet! I heard the bone snap when I hit the ground. It was horrible – made me feel sick. I couldn't use my arm at all after that, but Rostam seemed to think I was putting it on, even after the doctor told him I'd broken my collar bone."

Teriska Khan looked quite fierce.

"I always said it was mad for you to go off with Rostam. You're not used to this kind of life. You weren't brought up in the mountains, like Soran and Rostam. You can't be expected to . . ."

Ashti shook his head irritably.

"It's not like that, Mother," he said. "You don't understand. There are lots of students up there with the pesh murgas. I'm nothing special. It's just that, oh I don't know, just because I'm his nephew, Rostam seems to think I ought to be a hero, or superhuman or something, and I'm not, I can't, I . . ."

Ashti suddenly looked as if he was about to cry. He shook his head savagely and blinked hard. Tara couldn't bear it. She got up, picked up the water pot and went off to the spring. By the time she came home, Ashti seemed more like his old self, not the tough, daring pesh murga he'd been trying to become, but the studious, rather thoughtless but gentle brother he'd always been before.

Kak Soran didn't come home until the middle of the night. Tara hadn't been able to go to sleep. She was too aware of Ashti, tossing and turning uncomfortably, and grinding his teeth in his sleep. In the pitch darkness, she heard the door hinge creak as Kak Soran quietly opened it. Teriska Khan sat up.

"Shh! It's only me," Kak Soran said quietly.

Teriska Khan lay down again.

"Mind where you put your feet," she said. "Ashti's here."

Tara heard Kak Soran grunt with surprise.

"Why? What's happened?"

"He broke his collar bone in a mortar attack. Rostam was furious with him. He said . . ."

"Rostam's a fool. I should never have allowed him to take Ashti off with him. It's all very well being a hothead when you're twenty, but Rostam's thirty at least. He ought to know better by now. He takes too many risks. He's causing a lot of casualties. I know he's done some incredible things, but honestly . . ."

"Soran, I'm telling you straight, I don't want Ashti to go back to him."

Kak Soran didn't answer at once. Tara heard him bundle his clothes against the wall and sigh as he lay down, pulled a quilt over himself, and shifted round to find a comfortable position.

"Let's talk about it in the morning," he said sleepily.

But Teriska Khan had obviously worked up a head of steam. She packed so much feeling into her whisper that it came out as a hiss.

"We can't stay here forever! What are we going to do? Hero's terrified out of her wits every time she hears even a car or a truck in the distance. She thinks it's the planes coming back. We haven't had a single night without one of her bad dreams. I know Tara's doing her best, but she'll never take to village life, and anyway, it's not what we want for her. We could send her to Suzan, I suppose, in Baghdad, but I don't want to do that. We've just got to stay together! And look at Ashti. He'll never make a soldier. I don't mean he isn't brave, or doesn't try, or anything like that. He just hasn't got — oh, I don't know! If we can't go back home, to Sulaimaniya we'll have to . . . Well, I don't know what we'll do!"

Brought back unwillingly from the brink of sleep, Kak Soran turned over and sighed.

"Listen, Teriska. I didn't mean to tell you until tomorrow. I saw Fares Karwan today. He says they're going all out now to get the Kurdish leaders. They've executed at least three in the last week. Fares says even if the others don't die they'll never be the same again after what's been done to them. I tell you . . ."

"Don't," whispered Teriska Khan. "Please don't."

"Fares said I must move on as soon as possible. Too many people know I'm here. He . . ."

"Move on?" interrupted Teriska Khan.

"You know what I mean. Out of the country."

Tara heard Teriska Khan gasp.

"I could slip over the border into Iran on my own," Kak Soran went on. He seemed to be talking to himself, as if he was saying out loud for the first time things that had been going round and round in his mind. "It probably wouldn't be for too long, just until things have quietened down a bit. But the way things are going, I don't think they are going to quieten down. I can't leave you alone for long here with the girls. I've more or less made up my mind that we should all go. Now mind, Teriska, not a word of this . . ."

"What?" interrupted Teriska Khan in a frantic whisper. "Do you know what you're saying? We can't all go to Iran! We'd be refugees, without anything! How are we going to live? And what about all our things at home, the house and everything? We can't leave it all, just like that. Oh, why did you ever take all this on? Why did you have to . . ."

"That's enough," said Kak Soran sharply. "You know perfectly well . . ."

He stopped. Hero had started to thrash about, sighing and whimpering. Then she sat up, and began to cry.

"No! Stop them! Daya! Daya!"

Teriska Khan picked her up and rocked her.

"It's all right, my darling, go back to sleep. It's only a dream. Only a dream."

Hero cried for a bit longer, then groped around for her rabbit, and snuggled down again into her quilt.

"They bombed the next valley today," said Kak Soran. "Did you hear how many were killed? They went on until not a single house was left standing. Those villages just don't exist any more. It's only a matter of time before they come here again. If we go out we'll be refugees, but at least we'll be alive."

Teriska Khan didn't say anything.

"You've got to face up to it, Teriska," said Kak Soran. "We'll have to get out of the country. We couldn't have left without contacting Ashti, but now he's here we can go ahead. It's not as if we're the only ones. Thousands of Kurds have gone through into Iran. What do you want to do? Stay here so I can be executed and you can get blown up? We could do the journey all right. It's a long way, through the mountains, and you have to go by night, but there are good guides, and we'd have horses."

"But what about . . ." said Teriska Khan.

Kak Soran interrupted her with a huge yawn.

"Look," he said. "Do you mind? I've had about all I can take today. Let's get some sleep. We'll talk about it properly in the morning."

12

When Tara woke up the next morning, everything seemed the same as usual. Along with a few stray beams of sunlight, the ordinary early morning sounds of the village filtered through the badly fitting shutters. The wheezy old cock was complaining in his normal quavering crow. Out in the lane there was a sound of hooves slipping on stones and the crack of old Mustapha's stick on the rump of the mule that he was taking down the valley to fetch home a sack of flour. Baji Rezan's familiar laugh could be heard as she said hello to a neighbour on her way back from the spring. Teriska Khan was almost dressed, and was tying her scarf over her hair.

Then Tara remembered, and suddenly felt very wide awake. What had Baba said? They'd have to escape through the mountains to Iran? She thought she must have been dreaming. Baba and Daya couldn't possibly have said anything like that or they wouldn't be looking so calm and ordinary, yawning, and stretching and shaking out their bedding.

"Come on, darling," said Teriska Khan, seeing

Tara was awake. "Time to get up. Get the fire started. Baba's got to have his breakfast."

Kak Soran went outside to wash, but he stuck his head round the door again.

"I won't wait for tea. Just give me a bowl of yoghurt and some bread and cheese. I'd better get started at once."

"When will you want your dinner?" said Teriska Khan.

"How do I know?" said Kak Soran irritably. "Just get things ready." Teriska Khan looked up at him and nodded, and Tara knew they weren't talking about meals.

"So it's true," she thought, and a shiver like an icy finger ran down her spine. "We're going to Iran."

She pulled on her underdress and her long loose trousers, and slipped her feet into her sandals that lay by the door where she'd kicked them off last night. The sun was over the horizon already, and the early morning mist was disappearing from the last ravines and hollows in the hillsides. In the brilliant light the long spine of mountains to the east looked threatening.

Tara shivered. Why had she ever wanted to cross the mountains? She certainly didn't want to now. Going to Iran would mean leaving everything behind, everything she knew, home, school, friends, Granny, the special place under the oleander in the garden which had been her favourite hideout since she was little, old Mr Faris's shop in town where she and Leila had always gone to look for new records and posters, the fun of driving into Baghdad in the old black Mercedes to visit Auntie Suzan. At the moment, all that was only a few hours' drive away. Whatever Baba said about it being impossible and dangerous she could easily imagine herself just getting into a car and going back to it all. But if they went out, out of the country, she'd really be leaving everything behind, for ever, probably.

She tried to think of Iran, and the rest of the world beyond the mountains. She couldn't see anything. She couldn't even imagine anything. It was like staring into a black hole.

Behind her she heard a baby whining, and she turned round. Naman was holding tight round Ghazal's neck with one hand, while the fingers of the other were stuck into his mouth. He was sucking busily, and his little face was all screwed up.

Ghazal made a face.

"He's been awake half the night," she said. "Got a tooth coming through."

Naman saw Tara and suddenly gave a dazzling smile. He put out his arms to her. Tara tried to lift him off Ghazal's shoulder but as soon as she touched him, Naman changed his mind. His smile switched itself off, and he began to grizzle again, a long silver line of dribble running down his chin. He glared at Tara, as if he was daring her to touch him. Both girls laughed.

"Can you fix his pillow for me?" said Ghazal. "He won't let me put him down."

Ghazal's husband, on one of his rare visits home from the city where he worked, had fixed up a kind of swinging cradle from the lowest branch of the tree that grew up against Baji Rezan's house. Tara plumped up the cushion, shook out the blanket, folded it neatly and smoothed it onto the cradle.

Ghazal settled Naman down on it and pushed gently. The ropes were slung over a thick branch, and they creaked rhythmically as they rubbed against it. Naman suddenly gave a mighty yawn.

"I want to push it! Let me push!" Hero, still in her nightie and with her head all tousled, had heard the creaking ropes and came running up. Naman's cradle always worked like a magnet on her. She couldn't leave it alone. She'd even tried to climb into it once or twice, and had almost tipped Naman out into the dust.

"Don't touch it," said Tara, fending her off. "You'll push it too hard, like you did last time."

"I didn't!" said Hero indignantly. "Anyway, Naman liked it. He *likes* me! I push him *best*!"

"Well, push very gently then," said Tara.

Hero put one finger against the cradle and pressed. It barely moved.

"Can I leave him with you for a minute?" said Ghazal suddenly. "I want to go down to the pool and wash my hair, and my mother-in-law's gone to the fields already."

"Yes, of course," said Tara, feeling pleased. Ghazal hadn't left Naman with her before. She let Hero rock the cradle until he was fast asleep.

"Tara!" Teriska Khan called. "Come on! Breakfast's ready. What are you doing?"

"Go and tell her I'm minding Naman," said Tara to Hero, who was already bored with pushing. She scampered off round the corner of the house.

At that moment, without any warning, the bombers came again. Tara heard the explosions even before she heard the roar of the jets. She had no time to think, not a second in which to decide what to do. She just went for the nearest cover, and dived under Naman's cradle.

They'd gone almost as soon as they came, but Tara didn't dare come out in case they came back. She could hear feet running and people shouting in the lane on the other side of the courtyard wall, but it was as if she was paralysed. She couldn't move.

The bombers didn't come back, but Ghazal did. She burst into the courtyard, her long wet hair flying loose, shouting, "Naman! Naman!"

Tara self-consciously wriggled out from under the cradle and struggled to her feet. Ghazal bent over to snatch Naman up, then stopped herself. Naman was fast asleep, his eyelids fluttering gently as he dreamed.

"Well I never!" said Ghazal astonished. "Look at that! I don't believe it. All night long, if I only coughed or turned over he'd be awake and screaming at once, and he didn't even hear the planes!"

She began to giggle, and then, because she felt

so relieved, the giggles turned to roars of laughter.

Tara joined in dutifully, but she didn't feel like laughing at all. When the bombers had come, she hadn't tried to get Naman to safety. She'd even used his cradle to protect herself. She felt ashamed.

"I'd better go," she mumbled, and she sprinted off across the few yards that separated Baji Rezan's house from their own kitchen.

The bombs hadn't really done any damage to the village. They'd fallen wide, and all they'd managed to do was dig three craters in a field and kill a couple of goats. But though no one had been hurt, everyone felt a miserable increase in tension.

Teriska Khan seemed especially jumpy. She spent most of the day fussing over her clothes inside the house, sewing and sorting and snapping at Ashti, who obviously didn't feel like showing his face outside the courtyard walls, in case stories of what Rostam had said to him had got round the village, and people were laughing at him.

Tara was bored and restless. She was sitting under the apricot tree trying to teach Hero to play cat's cradle, when she heard sharp exclamations coming from inside the house.

"What's the matter, Daya?" Tara called out.

"My belt! I can't find my belt!" Teriska Khan called back.

Tara untangled her fingers, went to the door, and looked inside.

"Do you want me to help you?" she said.

"No! Don't come in here! Oh – yes, all right. Perhaps your young eyes – I must find it!"

Tara went into the house. It was unusually tidy. There were half-packed bags everywhere, and most of the clothes had been pulled out of the old wooden chest and were lying about in piles on the floor. Teriska Khan was searching through the bedding heaped up at the side of the room.

"It can't have fallen off when I was doing the washing yesterday! I'd have noticed at once. It's got to be in here somewhere. It must be! It *has* to be!"

Tara began to sift through a pile of Ashti's belongings.

"It's only a belt, Mother. Why . . ."

"Only! *Only!* You don't know what you're talking about."

Tara said nothing. With Daya in this mood, silence was the best course of action.

Teriska Khan was shaking out a folded blanket.

"It's not here! Oh, my God, it must be lost, or stolen . . ."

"Stolen?" Tara couldn't be quiet any longer. "But who on earth would want to steal your old belt?"

"It's not just an old belt! I've stitched half my jewellery into it! My gold necklace, and that heavy gold bracelet, and my ruby earrings – they're all in it!"

"Oh, I see."

Tara sat back onto her heels, frowning. She

was trying to remember everything that had happened when they'd gone to bed last night. She was sure she'd seen, just before the lamp went out, Teriska Khan folding her day clothes as she took them off and putting them down by the wall. Ashti had been asleep already, stretched out on his thin mattress, and he'd made the little room seem very crowded. When Baba had come in it hadn't been easy for him to find room for himself. Surely she'd heard him in the darkness moving some things onto the wooden clothes chest under the window, to give himself more space?

She went over to the window and pulled the chest out a couple of inches from the wall. She was right. The belt had fallen down behind it.

"Here it is," she said triumphantly, pulling it out and holding it up. Teriska Khan almost snatched it out of her hands.

"Oh, thank God!" she said. "How did you guess where it was?"

"I heard Baba move some stuff onto the chest when he came in last night."

"Oh." Teriska Khan paused. "Did you go to sleep straight away after that?"

"No."

"I see."

They looked at each other. Then Teriska Khan shrugged.

"Well, I don't see why you shouldn't know about it. It affects you as much as anyone. But you mustn't tell a soul. It's all got to be done in secret."

"When are we going?"

"I don't know. As soon as your father's got it all fixed up."

"Does Ashti know?"

"Not yet. Don't tell him. Baba will when he gets home."

Tara nodded.

"I'm scared, Daya."

"Me too," said Teriska Khan, "but I'm more scared of what they'll do to us if we stay here."

13

Two nights later, Tara woke up with a jerk. Someone was shaking her. She sat up, her heart thudding.

"Don't make a sound," whispered Kak Soran. "Just get up and put your clothes on. We're leaving."

Ashti was up already. He'd slept fully dressed, expecting to be woken up, and now he was trying to tie a strap round a bundle of bedding with his one good arm.

"Come and hold this for me," he said softly to Tara.

"Hang on a minute," she said, feeling around on the floor. "I can't find my clothes."

Teriska Khan heard her.

"Here, put these on," she said.

Tara felt something pushed into her arms, and then Kak Soran struck a match and lit the oil lamp. In its soft light Tara could see she was holding men's clothes, loose baggy trousers, a shirt, a long sash and a short sleeved jacket.

"But they're not . . ." said Tara.

"Just put them on," mouthed Teriska Khan

120

silently and she squatted down to help Ashti with his bundle.

Kak Soran had woken Hero and was trying to coax her into her sweater and trousers.

"Stop it! Go away!" she said irritably, in a loud clear voice that brought four hasty "Shsh" noises from the rest of the family.

Teriska Khan tucked in the end of the strap round Ashti's bundle and went over to sit beside her.

"We're going out," she said. "On a lovely horse. You like riding on horses. You're going with Baba and Daya and Ashti and Tara for a little journey."

Hero frowned up at her. She was trying so hard to think of something to say she didn't notice Kak Soran buckling her shoe onto her foot. She was holding her blue rabbit and its ears looked ridiculous, sticking up under her chin.

"My rabbit's not going on a journey," she said firmly. "He doesn't like horses. He's staying at home."

"Now come along, darling," said Teriska Khan in a cajoling voice. Hero wriggled out of the sleeve Kak Soran had just slipped over her arm. Her mouth had shut in an obstinate line and her chin was beginning to wobble.

"No," she said. "I won't."

Tara held her breath. It was obvious that Hero was building up to a tantrum. In a minute there'd be sobs and screams loud enough to wake the whole of Kurdistan.

Kak Soran stood up. He was a tall man, and in the light of the oil lamp, which cast long, deep shadows, he looked huge, even to Tara.

"Do what you're told, Hero," he said calmly. "Get up and put your sweater on. We're all going on a journey and we're not going to leave you behind."

He turned his back on her and bent over to pick up his felt waistcoat. Hero glared up at him for a moment, kicking her heels on the floor, then she saw he was taking no more notice of her, and she suddenly gave in.

Kak Soran was piling up by the door the cases and bags which Teriska Khan had been packing so carefully for the past few days.

"Do we really need all this stuff?" he said, holding up an oddly shaped bundle wrapped in a brightly printed cloth. "What's in this?"

"It's my samovar," said Teriska Khan defiantly, "and I'm not going anywhere without it."

Outside it wasn't as dark as Tara had expected. The moon was still up, and though it was only a half moon, it shone surprisingly brightly. It made the sleeping village, huddled against the steep hillside, look like a patchwork of deep shadows and faint splashes of grey.

Kak Soran hustled the family out of the house, took a last look round, picked up a sock that had fallen from a bag and tucked it into his pocket, then blew out the lamp. He pulled the door shut behind him, and turned the key in the padlock.

"Why bother, Father?" whispered Ashti. "What's the point? We're never coming back."

Kak Soran didn't answer. He lifted the two heaviest bags and went over to the door in the high wall of the courtyard. Tara picked up her share of the luggage and followed the others. She was the last to go through the gate. She turned back and looked at the two houses, their own and Baji Rezan's. They looked cosy, and familiar.

Just over the wall in the next courtyard a dog started barking, rattling its chain as it strained forward. As if they'd been waiting for a signal, every dog in the village began to bark too.

"Come on," whispered Kak Soran impatiently. Tara hurried out into the shadowy lane, stumbling on the loose stones, and he shut the door behind her.

There was an old walnut tree at the edge of the village and just as they got up to it, two men stepped out suddenly from the pitch dark shade under it. Tara jumped, but then she saw four horses and a mule, standing patiently with their heads lowered by the side of the path.

The guides were middle-aged men, and they looked as tough as their horses. They muttered something to Kak Soran, then began silently and efficiently to sort the baggage into balanced bundles of equal weight and lift them onto the backs of the mule and one of the horses, pulling at the straps and leaning heavily against the animals' flanks.

"He says we mustn't talk at all, not even in

whispers," Kak Soran said very softly to the rest of them. "The slightest sound travels for miles in the mountains. You never know who's watching and listening, and once we're near the top there'll be government troops in the watchtowers. They'll shoot at anything suspicious. The moon will have gone down by the time we get that far but if we're to slip past them without any trouble they mustn't hear a thing. Do you understand, Tara?"

Tara nodded indignantly. Of course she understood! It was Hero who was likely to cause problems. She didn't even know what the word 'silence' meant.

The pack horse and the mule were ready. The men seemed to be nervous, and one of them swore under his breath when a horse snorted loudly through its nostrils, and tossed its head so that the bit jingled.

"Get on," they said.

Kak Soran gave Tara a nudge, and she and Teriska Khan climbed onto the two biggest riding horses, while Kak Soran lifted Hero onto the back of the smallest, a stocky mountain pony. Luckily, Hero seemed to have accepted the situation. She obediently plumped down in the broad saddle and let Ashti take the reins.

They started off along the path away from the village. Tara couldn't understand at first why the horses' hooves didn't seem to be making the usual noise. She peered down at the feet of the pony in front. Its hooves looked big and bulky, and she realized they'd been wrapped in rags to muffle the sound.

The village dogs were still barking like mad, but there were no footsteps or voices. Anyone who'd woken up must have either decided to mind their own business, or thought that a jackal had come too close to the village, and set the dogs off.

A few minutes later the path had wound round the broad shoulder of the hill and the houses were out of sight.

For the first one or two miles the going wasn't too bad. Tara had been quite a long way down this path before. Years ago they'd all come out here for a picnic by that clump of willows over there near the stream. In that field she'd often watched the men winnowing the wheat after the harvest had been taken in. She used to love seeing the way they flicked basketfuls of seeds into the air, and she'd watch it spiral up in a golden shower, and the sunlight would catch on it, and the wind would blow away all the empty husks.

The track was broad, and reasonably flat. Tara had been on a horse before, but she felt a bit nervous at first in case this one was wild or temperamental. She soon realized she didn't have to worry. It was a lazy old thing, and she had to dig her heels into its sides from time to time to make it keep up with the others. Its hooves plopped softly onto the dusty path in a regular rhythm, and she started to imagine they were saying something, over and over again:

"Going out, going out, leaving home, leaving

home."

They'd left the house soon after midnight. By one or two o'clock the path was beginning to change. It was getting narrower. The fields and orchards were already behind them, and the ground was beginning to rise steeply. The moon had almost set now, but Tara could just see huge peaks towering up all around, with faint shimmers of snow on the jagged tops. Ahead there seemed to be nothing but a wall of rock.

They've made a mistake, she thought. They've taken the wrong path. We can't possibly get through that.

The moon sank behind a peak but in the last cold glimmer of light Tara could just make out a dark gash in the side of the mountain, and as they came up to it she could see that it was a cleft in the rock. Her horse followed the others into it.

She couldn't really see anything now, but from the way the sound of the horses' hooves had changed, she guessed they were surrounded by rock on all sides. From somewhere away to the right, down below, she could hear running water.

From now on, Tara didn't have time to think. The gorge was so dark she had to mind every step of the way. Hero had been surprisingly quiet for a long time, but she was getting restless now. She'd begun to chatter in a low voice, and had stopped taking any notice of Ashti, who kept telling her to be quiet. Her voice was getting louder and louder, until she suddenly called out, "Daya! Day—"

She stopped suddenly as Ashti jumped back

from the horse's head and whispered something savagely into her ear. After that she didn't say anything and Tara only heard a little dry cough, as she tried to clear all the dust out of her throat, or an occasional whimper when she came up against a branch or trailing root sticking out over the path.

Tara straightened her back and wriggled her shoulders to get the crick out of her neck. She was beginning to feel stiff and sore. She'd never been on horseback for as long as this before. The guide behind her seemed to be able to see in the dark. He came up quietly alongside her.

"Get off and lead your horse for a bit," he said softly, "but keep to the left of its head. There's a very steep drop down to the river from here on."

He slid past her and went on to pass the message to Ashti. Tara slipped off the horse's back, then nearly stumbled over her first few steps. Goodness, she was stiff! And she'd kicked a stone off the path! She listened for the rattle as it rolled down the hillside, but the rattle didn't come. The stone had fallen into thin air, and she had a horrible vision of it dropping over the edge of the precipice and plunging down for miles and miles into the river she could still hear far below. She shivered. The path was so narrow and uneven she could easily just step over the edge in the dark. She took a firmer grip on the horse's reins and hugged the steep rock wall on her left. A stone sticking out of it grazed her face, and a few minutes later she jumped as a tussock of grass brushed against her cheek, but she didn't dare move away from the side and further out into the path because she was so scared of the sheer drop on the other side.

The horse's head was right beside her shoulder, its sweet, hay-scented breath coming in even gusts. Once it stumbled, and went down on one knee. For a second she thought it had gone over the edge, but it righted itself again without any help from her. Although it was so dark, the horse seemed almost to know where it was going, as if it knew the path and had been this way hundreds of times before. Tara found it rather comforting.

She could hear the rushing noise of the water much more clearly now, and she guessed the drop down to the river was getting shorter. The path had been climbing less steeply for a while, and the riverbed had been coming up to meet it. Soon the roar was so loud that she couldn't hear the muffled tread of the horses ahead of her any more, and she didn't realize they'd stopped. She almost collided with the rump of Hero's pony.

"What's going on? What's happening?" she whispered to Ashti, who was standing beside her in the darkness.

"A bridge, I think," he answered. He sounded miserable. Tara wanted to squeeze his arm sympathetically, but she didn't dare. If she was unhappy, she thought, it was much worse for Ashti. He wasn't only leaving home, he was feeling a failure too. He was still brooding over his clash with Rostam.

The noise of the water covered the sound of voices, and the guides didn't seem to mind them talking here. Tara could hear Kak Soran, some way out to the right, leading Teriska Khan's horse, and she guessed they were on a bridge.

"Keep still now, for God's sake, don't fidget! Trust your horse to guide himself!" Tara had never heard Baba sound frightened before but he certainly sounded it now, and she felt a spasm of panic tighten her stomach.

Teriska Khan didn't usually pray out loud, but that's what she was doing.

"In the name of God the Compassionate," she was moaning through clenched teeth, "I take refuge from evil, I take refuge from evil!"

Now it was Ashti's turn to lead Hero's horse across. The water seemed to glow with a faint kind of luminous light, and Daya and Baba were on the other side. She'd be the last to cross, except for the second guide. She could hear Hero's shrill voice saying, "Don't cry, Rabbit. Don't be afraid. I'm looking after you. You're not allowed to cry, Rabbit. Stop it."

Then suddenly she felt a rough prod in the back from the guide behind her, and before she had time to think the narrow planks of the bridge were under her own feet. There was only a thin rope to hold onto on one side, and nothing at all on the other. Below, the water was boiling and raging around the rocks, almost spilling over the central section of the bridge. She could feel the spray on her hands and face.

She'd inched her way to the middle when she felt something suddenly swoop down near her head. There were bats diving around, snapping up insects over the water. They were almost getting tangled in her hair. She felt one flit past her cheek, and hit out at it. Her horse started back nervously and tossed its head up. Its hooves slithered on the swaying planks of the bridge. With a desperate effort, Tara steadied it, but it panicked, and bolted forward. She felt herself fall, and clutched at the hand rope, but she missed it, and plunged into the freezing water.

14

For the second time in a few weeks, Tara was quite sure she was going to die. The water was so freezing cold it made her feel numb all over, and she'd have been swept helplessly down the rapids below the bridge if she hadn't been tossed against a large rock. She lashed out with both arms and managed to get a grip on it. She wasn't frightened now. She was just furiously angry. She wouldn't let this stupid river kill her! She wasn't going to give in to anything or anyone!

She didn't have much time to think. The water was tugging at her, and the current was so strong she knew she couldn't hold on for long. She pressed herself against the slippery surface of the rock as hard as she could, and screamed.

Ashti heard her. The others, except for the second guide, had already started off up the path, but Ashti came running back onto the bridge and pushed aside the guide who was peering helplessly downstream in the direction in which Tara had disappeared.

Ashti kicked off his shoes, gave them to the guide and deliberately lowered himself off the bridge and into the river, holding onto one of the planks with his good hand. The water came up to his chest.

Although he'd only been with the pesh murgas for a short while, Ashti had had to cross quite a few dangerous rivers and even in the dark he could sense the way this one was running. Just below the bridge there was a kind of pool, and the water swirled and eddied round it, racing towards a narrow channel at the top of a long run of rapids. The current was terrific, and it was especially bad where Tara was, right at the entrance to the channel where the water was running fastest.

Tara knew her only hope was to keep on shouting and screaming till someone came to help her, but it seemed ages before she heard Ashti answering.

"Hang on!" he yelled. "I'm coming!"

The rocks at the bottom of the pool were slippery, and even though he desperately wanted to hurry, Ashti had to make himself go carefully, feeling his way step by step so that he wouldn't be knocked off his feet and get carried away too.

He got to her at last, after what seemed like a lifetime to both of them. Even though she could hear him, and just see him now, Tara was still screaming. He edged round to the quietest side of the rock she was clinging to, out of the main race.

"Shut up," he said. "Take my hand."

She had to let go of the rock to reach for him. In the darkness their hands almost missed each other, but then he caught hold of her wrist and now he was managing to steady her against the current.

"You'll just have to throw yourself towards me," he said, panting.

She tried to, but her foot slipped and she suddenly disappeared under the water. She went down so fast she almost knocked Ashti off his feet but he just managed to hang on, and heaved at her wrist, leaning backwards against the current. Her lungs seemed to be bursting, but she scrabbled along the river bed with her free hand, inching towards him, and then she came up right in front of his face.

They were on the edge of the mainstream now, working their way towards the edge of the pool. Tara wondered what the awful pain in her wrist was, and then she realized that Ashti's hand was still round it, as strong as a vice. He was towing her behind him.

"Wait a minute!" she said. "Isn't the bridge that way?"

"We'll never get back up onto it," he said. "The bank's over here, and the water's slow this side. Just follow me and keep quiet. We've made too much noise already."

They weren't the only ones to make a noise. Tara could hear Daya's voice now. She'd cast caution to the winds and was practically shouting.

"For Heaven's sake, Soran, you mustn't go in! You can't! Think of Hero and me! You won't be able to see a thing! You don't know what direction they're in. You can't even swim! Oh my God, why ever did we leave the village? Ashti! Tara! Where are you? Can you hear me?"

One of the guards interrupted her.

"Keep your voice down, missus, can't you? We don't want any more trouble on top of this. The river's high today, after the storm this morning. They'll have gone down the rapids. Don't give up hope. They might get out all right lower down. We'll keep an eye open for them on our way back."

"Baba! Daya!" gasped Tara. She heard Teriska Khan's shout, "Listen! I heard something!" then feet came scrambling down the bank towards the water's edge.

"Where's Ashti?" said Kak Soran, straining his eyes to see past Tara.

"Here," said Ashti, splashing out of the water, and Tara could hear his teeth chattering as loudly as her own.

"Oh God, oh thank God!" said Teriska Khan. She was crying and laughing at once. Tara couldn't say anything. She was trembling so violently with the cold that she could hardly move.

"You must change! You've got to get out of these wet clothes!" said Teriska Khan. "Which bag are your things in? We'll have to find you something dry – "

The guards had been talking to Kak Soran who came up to Teriska Khan, took her elbow, and steered her firmly back to her horse.

"There's no time," he said quietly, slipping off his felt waistcoast. "We're an hour behind already. Look, Tara, wring out as much water as you can, then take off your coat and sash and put mine on. Your trousers will just have to dry on you. Don't ride for a bit. Walk and swing your arms to get warm. Come on – we really mustn't stay here any longer."

Tara nodded in the dark, too cold to reply. She wrapped Kak Soran's sash round herself and struggled into his coat. Ashti had started up the path already, and he was quickly climbing the hill with the first guide. He'd even refused to take the blanket off Hero's saddle to wrap round himself. He'd proved he wasn't short of courage to everyone else, but he still seemed to be trying to punish himself.

The climb was hard work now. The path went up and up, and was almost as steep as a staircase in some places. And though they'd left the river behind, so that there was no steep drop on one side, they still weren't out of danger. In one way it was worse. They couldn't count on the sound of running water to cover up any noises they might make. It was scary how loudly the rattling of a stone, or the whinnying sneeze of a horse echoed from rock to rock in the thin mountain air.

The climb to the pass between the two highest peaks at the crest of the mountain range was exhausting, but Tara didn't really mind. For one thing, having to work so hard warmed her up.

For another, she was just enjoying the feeling of being alive. She'd cheated death for the second time. It made her feel powerful, as if she'd sort of died, and her life had started all over again. And then she couldn't stop thinking about how Ashti had jumped into the river to come after her, even though he still had a broken collar bone. He'd risked his life for her.

Granny and Daya were right, she thought. She'd often heard them say, "the family must come first, we've got to stick together," and she'd never really understood what they meant. Now she knew.

"I'll never tease you or laugh at you or show you up again, Ashti," she promised silently.

The path was twisting and turning like a switchback now, up a slope of rough, treacherous scree. The guide in front stopped and passed a whisper back to everyone. There was a watchtower full of soldiers not far away, somewhere over to the left. This was the most dangerous bit of the whole journey.

Tara looked anxiously at the sky. She'd been longing for the dawn all night, but now it was nearly here she wished it would hold off for an hour or two. The darkness had already begun to turn into a dim grey over the ridge of rock up ahead. She could see clearly the sharp edge of the hill top above. She could see something else, too. A little way above and to the left, looking rather messy like Haji Laqlaq's nest, was a ramshackle sort of building. It seemed completely out of place here in these wild savage mountains. The more she looked at it the more easily she could make it out. That was where the soldiers were, waiting and watching, supposed to be stopping anyone from getting up the paths that criss-crossed the ridges below.

A bit further back they'd passed a few patches of snow, which the spring sun hadn't been strong enough to melt, and the higher they climbed the deeper it got, until it was banked up on both sides, quite deep in some places where it had drifted, but blown off the bare rock in others. Tara's feet were so cold she couldn't feel her toes any longer, and now that it was really getting light she could see that her breath was coming out in frosty puffs in front of her face.

Her trousers were still horribly wet and clammy, and they were rubbing uncomfortably against the insides of her legs. She tried to forget about them. She had to be really on the alert now, keep an eye on Hero, watch where she put her feet, and make sure she was leading her horse over the smoothest places so it wouldn't stumble again.

They seemed to creep up the exposed hillside incredibly slowly, and it seemed to be getting lighter incredibly quickly.

Just – keep – going, thought Tara, gritting her teeth.

Behind her the second guide was leading Hero's horse, while Hero herself was being carried up the last slope on Kak Soran's shoulders, where she was apparently asleep. Suddenly, Tara saw a bit of blue fluff fall out of her arms. Hero had dropped her rabbit. She woke up with a jolt, and opened her mouth to wail but Tara darted forward, scooped up the mass of blue fluff and stuck it back in Hero's arms before she'd had time to let out a squeak.

Tara had been living for the moment when they'd safely reach the top of the spur they were climbing. But when she got there, she was disappointed. There wasn't even a view on the other side. The path just meandered on in a boring undramatic way, still going up and zigzagging between tumbled rocks and old packed snow. The best that could be said of it was that the watchtower was way behind them, and out of sight.

Then, all of a sudden, they turned another corner, dipped down and up over an ice-filled hollow and at the top of the very last rise, as the first rays of the sun hit them full in the face, they found they were looking down and down over a vast plain, falling away from the mountains.

"Iran," said Teriska Khan softly.

Behind and on either side, the jagged peaks of the Zagros stretched away as far as the eye could see, but there was a steep path straight ahead running down to a smoother slope which in the bright, early morning sun looked pretty much the same as the valley of their village on the other side.

"But it's like . . ." Tara called across to Kak

Soran, then she clapped her hand over her mouth.

He grinned at her, and she could see that he was tremendously relieved. Hero was still up on his shoulders. She lifted her head but decided not to wake up, and buried it back again in Kak Soran's neck.

"Don't worry," he called back to Tara. "We're over the border. The guards are all behind us. We can talk now. Yes, you're quite right. Of course this is like our side. It ought to be. It's still Kurdistan."

In front of him, Ashti snorted sarcastically.

"Fine Kurds we are! Look at us! Running away, giving up . . ."

"Ashti," Kak Soran said, with a sort of patient resignation, "don't talk rubbish. Did you really imagine that we left Iraq because we're giving up the struggle?"

"What do you mean?" said Ashti. He looked awful. His clothes were still wet, his injured shoulder was hunched up awkwardly as if it was hurting badly and he was obviously exhausted.

"Guns and bombs aren't the only weapons, whatever Rostam's been telling you," Kak Soran said drily. "I was never cut out to be a soldier myself. You're the hero in this family, you idiot, plunging into that river in the dark, with one useless arm, to pull Tara out."

Ashti went red.

"This is my weapon," Kak Soran tapped his head with his forefinger. "Brains, Ashti. Words. Pens rather than swords. It's about time the rest

139

of the world knew about what's going on over there." He jerked his finger towards the mountains behind.

"But . . ." said Ashti.

Tara stopped listening. She'd looked back when Baba had pointed towards the mountains. The sun was properly up now, and the walls of rock looked so massive, so black and so frightening that she couldn't believe they'd come all the way through them.

"They're like huge gates," she thought, "locked and barred, and we're on the wrong side."

Suddenly she felt extremely tired and hungry. She pulled on the reins of the horse she was still leading to bring it up to her, and climbed onto it. The path was easier now. It would be a comfortable ride all the rest of the way.

15

The first sign that showed Tara they really were in a foreign country was an Iranian flag fluttering from a high pole above a huddle of low buildings. As soon as it came into view the guides stopped the horses. One started quickly unloading the pack horse and the mule. The other helped Teriska Khan to dismount. She stumbled when her feet touched the ground and she had to lean against the horse's flank, trying to stand.

"Get off," said Kak Soran to Tara. "The guides have got to go back now."

The two men were swearing over the difficult knots in the ropes and they kept looking back down the road that led to the village. Tara could see why they were worried. Some Iranian soldiers were running up the road towards them.

If Tara hadn't already escaped from the secret police by the skin of her teeth over the garden wall, lived through two bombing raids and almost been drowned in a freezing river in the middle of the night, she'd have been frightened almost to death at the sight of soldiers from an enemy country hurrying towards her with guns in their hands. As it was, she just hoped they'd take her somewhere where she could have something to eat and then go to sleep.

The guides were halfway up the slope before the soldiers arrived. Tara could still hear them urging their tired horses back up into the shelter of the mountains, where they'd rest them for the day in a deserted valley and then slip back over to the other side after dark. The soldiers didn't try to follow them. They surrounded the exhausted family and one of them, who was obviously an officer, rattled off a lot of questions in Persian.

Kak Soran spread out his hands and shook his head to show that he didn't understand.

"Kurdish," he said.

The officer tutted irritably, and nodded to them to pick up their bundles and follow him. The young Iranian soldiers stood watching while Kak Soran and Ashti picked up the largest bags and Teriska Khan and Tara struggled with all the smaller ones.

Kak Soran had put Hero down. She was still half asleep. She clutched at Teriska Khan's skirt.

"Daya carry me," she said. Teriska Khan put her bags down and picked her up. Tara stood there hesitating. She couldn't carry any more, but she didn't want to leave the bags lying on the ground.

The officer watched impatiently, and then he spoke to one of the soldiers who picked up the remaining bags, and they all set off down the hill.

The largest building in the little group of

houses was obviously some kind of army post. The officer gestured to them to put their baggage down on the rough dusty ground outside the door. A man with a beard was squatting there with his back resting against the wall. He had a string of beads in one hand and he was running them through his fingers. Apart from his hands he didn't seem to move at all. He just sat watching everything that went on with his one good eye. Where the other eye had been there was nothing but a dent in his face with the lids closed over it.

The officer went inside the building, and the family followed him. He sat down at the desk that faced the door, and said something to the clerk who'd followed him in. The clerk looked up. His eyes slipped past Teriska Khan and settled on Tara. She felt suddenly hot and uncomfortable, and turned her back to look out through the open door across the rooftops of the village. Smoke was curling up from cooking fires, and the thought of people making breakfast made her feel hungrier and thirstier than ever.

Apart from the officer's desk and chair the room was practically empty except for a couple of battered benches along the two side walls, and a large framed photograph of the Ayatollah above the officer's desk.

Teriska Khan couldn't stand any longer. She sank down on one of the benches with a sigh of exhaustion, and leant her head against the peeling blue paint. Under all the dust on her face Tara could see that she was very pale.

"I'm hungry," said Hero. "I want a drink."

She climbed onto Teriska Khan's knee and began to jiggle up and down. For once, Teriska Khan didn't take much notice of her. Kak Soran managed to catch the officer's eye and he pointed to Hero and mimed lifting a cup to his mouth. The officer nodded, and said something to the clerk, who went outside with a last sidelong look at Tara.

An hour later, they were still sitting there, watching and waiting. All kinds of men, some in soldier's uniform and some in ordinary clothes had been coming and going. One after the other they sat down on the old wooden chair in front of the officer's desk and chatted to him. At first Tara tried to listen to their rapid Persian, and make some sense of it, but she soon gave up. It was no good. She couldn't understand a word.

The clerk came back in the end with a jug of water, and some hunks of dry stale bread. They were all so thirsty that the water tasted wonderful, and as soon as they'd drunk they tried to eat the bread, but after a couple of bites Teriska Khan gave up and shut her eyes again. Tara nudged her.

"Daya," she said, "didn't you pack some food? Why don't we open it now?"

Teriska Khan nodded but didn't make a move towards the bags. Tara looked nervously at the officer, and untied one of the bundles. She pulled out some of Teriska Khan's own, much better bread, a bit of fresh goat's cheese and a few sweet cakes, and handed them surreptitiously to Hero and Kak Soran.

"Here, Daya," she said, putting a piece of bread in Teriska Khan's hand. Teriska ate a few mouthfuls, then started coughing.

"What's going to happen?" whispered Tara. "What'll they do with us?"

No one answered.

"If they don't deal with us soon," said Ashti savagely, "I'll – "

"Be quiet, Ashti," said Kak Soran. "Don't forget, we're refugees. We're in their hands. They can do whatever they like with us, so there's no point in aggravating them. Just keep cool. They won't keep us here forever."

At long last, they heard a car pull up outside. Tara looked out of the open door. A middle-aged captain was climbing out of a jeep, driven by a young soldier. He marched into the army post. The man behind the desk jumped smartly to his feet and saluted, and the one-eyed man with the beads, who was still squatting beside the wall and didn't seem to have moved a muscle, stood up, and slouched inside.

The captain said something to him, and the one-eyed man turned to Kak Soran and said in Arabic, "Open your bags."

Tara and Ashti looked at each other. Who was this person? Did he speak Kurdish as well as Arabic? Had he been listening all this while, hoping to pick up something from their conversation?

"The captain says to open your bags," the one-eyed man said again.

Kak Soran bent down and began to untie the straps round one of the bags. The captain saw Tara and Teriska Khan standing against the wall. He frowned and said something under his breath.

"He says to cover your heads," said the one-eyed man indifferently. Tara felt herself blushing scarlet! He must have thought she was a tramp or something. Of course, they were like that in Iran, really strict about women's clothes. If you weren't covered with a veil from head to foot they assumed you were a prostitute, and you could even get put in prison for it. She felt dreadfully self-conscious. It wasn't only that her scarf had slipped off and got lost somewhere on the journey, she'd never looked such a mess in her life. For a start she was wearing men's clothes, and then on top of that she'd been soaked to the skin and covered with dust. As for her hair – !

Quickly she dived into the bag Kak Soran had opened, pulled another scarf out, put it over her head and tied it with a knot at the back.

"Not like that," said the one-eyed man. "Under your chin. You mustn't show any hair at all. You should have a proper chador. The captain wants to know why you aren't wearing one."

"Chador?" said Tara.

"A veil, to cover yourself up with."

"Oh! I – we – "

The one-eyed man didn't wait for her to answer. He spoke to the captain in Persian, who rapped out an order to the clerk. The clerk smiled in a way that Tara didn't like at all, and went out again.

The captain settled himself in the chair behind the desk. He pointed to the one in front of it and nodded to Kak Soran. The one-eyed man, who was obviously going to be the interpreter, pulled up another chair and sat down too.

The younger officer who'd first met them was searching through their bags, looking in every pocket of every garment, and feeling in every fold of every blanket. Teriska Khan hardly seemed to notice what was going on, but Tara was following every move and trying not to show how tense she really was. The officer stopped at last and stood up. Tara tried not to let a triumphant smile break out all over her face.

Hero was asleep again. She was curled up on the bare floor, as deeply relaxed as if she were in her own bed at home.

"Lucky her," thought Tara.

The three-way conversation between Kak Soran, the captain and the one-eyed man was making her feel uncomfortable. For one thing, how could anyone know if the translator was doing his job properly? He might be saying anything, making up all kinds of lies about them.

For another thing, the questions were so stupid. The captain kept asking the same things over and over again, going round and round in circles.

"Who are you? What's your name? Where do you come from? Why have you left Iraq? Why are

147

you here? What's your profession? Is this your wife? Are these your children? Where do you live? Who are you? What's your name?"

Tara had never seen her father treated like this before. He'd always been the person in charge, and people had always come to him to ask his advice, and listen respectfully to his opinions. Now he was sitting forward on the edge of his chair, as if he was begging a favour or something, and he had a humble tone in his voice that made her feel ashamed.

The clerk came back after a long time with two pieces of black cloth over his arm. He gave one to Tara and one to Teriska Khan who took hers without a word, and draped it over her head and round her shoulders. Tara copied her, trying to seem just as unconcerned and dignified. The shiny material was a cheap polyester, and it wasn't easy to stop it slipping off the back of her head. She had to keep yanking it back into place.

She felt very, very tired. She leaned her head against the stained, peeling wall, and felt her eyelids drop, but every time she slipped into a doze, her head lolled uncomfortably forwards or sideways, and she woke up with a jerk, to find the wretched chador had slipped off again and the clerk was staring at her.

It was midday when at last the endless questions seemed to be over. The clerk had brought in a tray of tiny tea glasses and even Hero, who'd woken up and was very cross, seemed to feel a bit better after she'd drunk a couple of warm sweet glasses.

In the end the captain seemed to be as bored with the interrogation as the interpreter obviously was. He stood up, stretched, and came round to the front of the desk to look down at the mess the younger officer had made of the baggage. Teriska Khan's careful packing was tossed all over the dusty concrete floor in a jumble of clothes, cooking utensils, jars, packets of food and washing things which were all mixed up together.

"He says to pack it all up," said the interpreter, yawning, "and be quick because the car's waiting."

The driver of the jeep that had brought the captain didn't seem to be in much of a hurry to go. He'd moved out of the hot morning sun into the shade of a tree, and was sitting over a backgammon board with some other soldiers. But the captain was suddenly in a tremendous hurry. He gave them no time to fold the clothes or wrap up the breakables, but stood watching impatiently while Tara, Ashti and Kak Soran hastily shoved everything back into the bags.

Tara kneeled down to do the packing, but she found her chador kept getting in the way. Every time she let go of it and leaned forward to use both hands it slid off her head, and when the bags were finally done up again, and she stood up, she accidentally trod on a corner of it and it fell off onto the floor in a heap.

"Put it on, quick," said Ashti, his tired face red with anger. "If that disgusting little clerk looks at you again I'm going to bash his head in."

It was a squash in the jeep. The captain sat in front with the driver and the rest of them squeezed into the back with the bags.

"Where are we going? I want to go home! I want to go home!" cried Hero, saying out loud what they were all thinking. The road was rough and full of potholes and they were shaken around on the old jeep's worn springs as if they were riding a bucking horse.

The journey lasted half an hour but nobody said much. Tara was facing the back window but she could hardly see anything because of the clouds of dust that swirled up behind the jeep. It seeped in through every crack round the windows, and made her throat feel rough and dry.

She was beginning to feel carsick, and as though every bone in her body was bruised, when at last they pulled up at the edge of another village. This one was bigger than the last, with more soldiers, and a larger army compound. There were military vehicles parked in an orderly row behind whitewashed lines, and the Iranian flag fluttered from a tall flagpole above the main building.

The captain got out, and strode off round the corner and out of sight. The driver switched off the engine.

"What do we do now?" burst out Ashti. "Wait? Sit here forever? Hope someone takes pity on us eventually?"

"I think we should get out of this jeep anyway," said Kak Soran, ignoring Ashti's outburst. "I want to stretch my legs."

A few minutes later a soldier appeared. Tara quickly pulled her chador well up over her hair and round her face. She didn't want anyone else to stare at her like that awful clerk had done. The soldier jerked his head to show that they were to follow him. Once more they picked up all their bags and bundles and followed him to a low building at the far end of the compound with two rooms, both opening onto a verandah, and with no interlinking door.

The soldier opened one of the doors, and Kak Soran went in. Tara tried to follow him but the soldier frowned and put out an arm to stop her. He took Ashti by the shoulder, and pushed him in after his father, then he opened the door to the second room and nodded to Teriska Khan and Tara.

"Men and women are to be separate," sighed Kak Soran. "Well, at least we're not far away from each other."

Tara was desperate to lie down and go to sleep. She ducked her head under the low doorway and went into the women's room. It was a small room, and it seemed full of people, although there were only three women and a child of six or seven in it. They were sitting against one of the bare walls, looking warily at the newcomers.

"Go in," said Teriska Khan behind Tara. "What are you waiting for?"

The women heard and they all began nodding and smiling.

"Oh, are you Kurdish too?" the oldest one said eagerly. "Have you just come over the mountains from Iraq? We arrived two days ago. What a terrible journey! Come in and sit down. You look exhausted."

"Yes, we are," said Teriska Khan faintly.

"We're starving too," said Tara.

"They'll bring us something to eat later on. It didn't come yesterday till after four o'clock," the same woman said, "but we've got a few olives and some bread and fruit here. You're very welcome to it. Go on, Fatimah, get it out."

The food wasn't much but it was better than nothing, and it was so lovely to be with friendly people from home, who were Kurds and refugees too, that Tara started to feel a bit more cheerful.

"Where do you come from?" said Fatimah eagerly to Tara.

"Sulaimaniya," said Tara, stifling a gigantic yawn.

Fatimah laughed.

"Why don't you lie down and go to sleep?" she said. "We'll have lots of time to talk later."

"Thanks," mumbled Tara. She lay down right where she was, a piece of half-eaten bread in her hand, and fell fast asleep at once.

16

Tara slept all the rest of the afternoon, all evening and all night, though she woke up enough to have a good supper that the other family kindly cooked for them with the rations they'd been given. When she finally woke up properly next morning, she was so stiff she groaned. The rough concrete floor was covered only by a dirty mat, and it hadn't made a comfortable bed, but she'd been too exhausted to notice.

She was trying to drag a comb through her tangled hair when she heard loud voices from the men's quarter next door. The captain was shouting furiously, and he hardly stopped for long enough to let the interpreter translate. Kak Soran only gave a few answers, and when he did speak he sounded slow and stupid, quite unlike his usual self.

Teriska Khan was still asleep. Tara jumped up and went to the door.

"Don't forget your chador!" one of the other girls said, scrambling after her with the piece of black cloth.

Tara opened the door and peeped out, trying to hear without being seen, but Kak Soran and the interpreter were speaking quietly and their voices sounded confused. All she could catch was Ashti's name, but she didn't hear Ashti's voice.

After a while the captain seemed to burn himself out. Kak Soran's quiet answers and his convincing show of stupid bewilderment seemed to calm him down. He shrugged his shoulders and marched off, swinging his arms in a soldierly way. Tara darted out to catch her father before he went back into the men's quarter.

"What's happened? What was all that about Ashti?"

"He ran off in the night. He's gone back to the mountains."

"Oh no! How awful! What will Daya say?"

"What's all this about?" Tara turned. Teriska Khan had woken up and was standing behind her. She had one hand pressed to the side of her head as if she had a headache.

"Ashti ran away in the night," said Tara.

"Oh, my God! Oh no!" Teriska Khan pushed Tara aside. "Why did you let him go?"

"Listen." Kak Soran was feeling bad himself. He wasn't in the mood to argue with his wife. "Do you know what they told me in there?" he said, nodding towards the open door behind him, through which Tara could see a group of other Kurdish men, all sitting in silence round the walls. "They told me some Iraqi Kurdish boys have been sent to join the Iranian army! If Ashti was here

154

he'd have to fight for Iran. Think of that – he might have to kill some of our own people! And if he refused do you know what they'd do?"

Teriska Khan shuddered.

"Where's he gone? What's he going to do?"

"He's gone back to Rostam. It was the only thing he could do. He had all night to travel in, and he slept all yesterday afternoon so he was pretty well rested. He'll have arrived back at the village we first came to hours ago. There were more guides coming through again last night with another lot of refugees. I heard ours talking about it. He'll meet them above the village, hide and sleep with them today and go back over tonight."

Teriska Khan didn't say anything, and Tara knew she was crying. Kak Soran said roughly,

"Don't make a big thing of it. It'll work out all right. You saw what Ashti was like yesterday. He can't cope with this kind of thing, being ordered around by other people. It would be even more dangerous for him here. He'd do something silly, lose his temper, or get into a fight, or something. And if they did send him off to join the Iranian army what hope would there be for him? They'd watch an Iraqi Kurd like a hawk. One false move and they'd do for him. Anyway, they'd probably send him straight to the front, where the casualties are highest. Don't you see? This was the only way out for him. I should never have let him come with us in the first place."

"But he hasn't got any food or money or anything!"

"He had an enormous dinner last night. You should have seen him eat! There's about seven or eight of them in there, and they gave him a good send-off, I can tell you! They'd be going back themselves if it wasn't for their families. And I gave him some money, enough to pay the guides, and something over for emergencies. I know you don't have much faith in Rostam, but he is Ashti's uncle. He may have bawled him out once or twice, but he'll look after him."

Teriska Khan didn't seem particularly comforted by the thought of Rostam, but she didn't try to argue.

"He never said goodbye to me," she said sadly.

Kak Soran smiled. She'd obviously accepted the inevitable. He was relieved.

"Did you want him to get the whole barracks up? Make a big scene of it? Of course he couldn't say goodbye to you. But he went off looking happy. I think he regretted leaving the pesh murgas all the time. You know what he's been like since he left Rostam. As miserable as a jackal in a cage. Well, last night he was his old self again. 'Tell her not to worry about me,' he said."

One of the men inside the room called out a warning. Kak Soran looked up. Two soldiers were looking across in their direction.

"Get back inside," said Kak Soran quickly. "We're not supposed to talk. I told the captain I had no idea what Ashti was planning to do. I think he believed me, but he's still suspicious. And mind what you say in front of the others.

However friendly they are, the less they know the better."

Tara was longing to talk it all over with Daya, but Teriska Khan didn't seem up to talking. She sank down against the wall.

"Are you all right, Daya?" said Tara. "You don't look very well. There's some food left over from last night. Would you like me to get you some?"

One of the older women had been watching. She came over and picked up Teriska Khan's hand.

"Your mother's got a touch of fever," she said. She arranged a blanket on the floor. "Lie down here and rest. She's exhausted, poor soul, and no wonder."

The day passed slowly. Teriska Khan slept most of the time. They were only allowed to go out to the smelly old latrines round the back of the building, and there was nowhere they could have a proper wash. Worst of all, no one knew what was going to happen next. As the morning passed, and the afternoon wore on, Tara began to feel they might be here in this cramped little room for ever.

Someone came at last when it was nearly evening. It was the interpreter. He told Kak Soran to follow him to the main office. A few minutes later, Kak Soran hurried back with news.

"They're taking us on somewhere else," he called in through the door of the women's quarters. "Get the bags ready. They're coming for us soon."

"Where are we going?" Tara called back.

"They won't say. To a refugee camp of some kind, I think."

"But what . . ." began Tara.

A soldier standing nearby shouted something.

"We'd better not talk any more," said Kak Soran. "Just start packing. Be as quick as you can. We'd better not keep them waiting or they might leave us behind."

Not knowing was the worst thing, thought Tara. It made you feel so helpless. She hadn't expected things to be like this. They'd left Iraq with only one thought, to get away to safety. Then the journey had been so difficult and dangerous that they'd had no time to think about what it would be like once they arrived.

She'd vaguely thought that, once they were in Iran, they'd go to Teheran, and her father would find a job, and she'd go to school, and they'd find a kindergarten for Hero. They'd have to learn Persian of course, and they'd have less money than before. The house would be smaller, and it wouldn't be easy making new friends, but still, they'd make a go of it, as long as they were all together. Baba had been to Iran before, a few years ago. He knew people in Teheran, and he even had some distant cousins there. When the war was over, of course, they'd go home.

The other women were talking excitedly, bundling their things together. They were like the women from the village. In fact, they looked as if they'd never left their village before. They didn't look as if they'd have any contacts in Iran, or any money to get started with.

"Perhaps it's only them going on to the refugee camp," thought Tara. "We'll probably be taken on to Teheran."

An hour later, when it was nearly dark, a minibus pulled up outside the two roomed building. Everyone was told to get in. There was no chance to object or ask questions. The captain himself was in charge of their departure. Tara lugged the bags outside, and Kak Soran took them from her.

"Daya's not very well, Baba," said Tara.

Kak Soran looked surprised. Though he had occasional fevers and viruses himself, Teriska Khan never seemed to go down with anything.

"She's tired and upset, I expect," he said. "Get a move on and make sure you put your chador on. There's no sense in offending them."

"But we're not going to this camp place, are we?" said Tara.

"It'll only be temporary I expect," said Kak Soran. "Better do what they say."

The minibus was old, but at least it had proper springs. The interpreter and a soldier sat in the front with the driver. Tara sat by a window. This time she wouldn't be staring out of the back into a cloud of dust, but she still wouldn't see much except what the minibus's headlights picked up.

The first hour was all right. Hero had recovered as if by magic from the awful journey through the mountains, and she started showing off and clowning. She made everyone laugh, and even the interpreter turned round and smiled. But in the end she climbed onto Teriska Khan's knee.

"Can you take her, Tara?" said Teriska Khan. "I've got such a headache."

Tara patted her knee invitingly. Hero pulled a face and started to object, but Tara picked her up, and settled her into her arms. Hero bounced around for a moment or two, then cuddled in and started sucking her thumb, which meant she'd soon be asleep.

Once she was quiet, they all fell silent. It wasn't a friendly, relaxed silence, but a tense, uneasy one. It was so strange and frightening not knowing where they were, or where they were going, not even knowing the names of the towns they passed through. Tara was glad she was holding Hero. Her curled up body felt warm and relaxed and comforting.

Kak Soran and the other men talked quietly together on the middle seats. Tara heard a bit of what they were saying.

"Not allowed to work here? But surely . . . my cousin . . . five years ago . . . a good job in Tabriz."

"Yes, but . . . before the war . . . Kurds suspected . . ."

She couldn't catch all they said. The roar of the engine was too loud. She stopped listening, and soon she fell into a kind of doze, half dreaming, half awake.

She was at home again. It would be the summer holidays now. She and Leila were planning to invite a party of their school friends. Khadijah would come of course, and Nasreen, who was so shy she hardly ever spoke to anyone. She'd ask Daya to help her make honey cakes, and they'd play their favourite records and try on a few clothes. Perhaps they were all doing it right now, without her. Did they think of her at all? Did they miss her?

She opened her eyes. She didn't want that dream to go on any longer. It was too uncomfortable. Instead, she'd imagine that the minibus was going in the opposite direction, south-west instead of north. It was driving towards Sulaimaniya through the pleasant rolling countryside of northern Iraq on a bright morning, past fields full of early ripening wheat and nodding sunflowers. It would soon stop in front of the house. Baba would unlock the door. They'd all rush in. She'd dash straight to the bathroom, have a long shower, wash her hair and change into some clean clothes. She'd never felt so filthy in her life.

After a while the daydreams faded and Tara's mind went blank. Without really seeing it, she watched the dusty verge of the road, lit up in the minibus's headlights, flashing hypnotically past. Every now and then they'd pass a brief blaze of light that streamed out from an open mosque door, or from the square window of a village house. Occasionally they went through a larger town where she caught sight of a busy bus station and a crowded main street.

After what seemed like hours and hours, the minibus began grinding its way up a steep mountain road. It was so winding that Hero would have been sick if she hadn't been fast asleep, slumped against Tara's shoulder.

"What's the time?" Tara whispered, not liking to break the silence. Kak Soran squinted at his watch.

"Two o'clock. This can't go on much longer. We must be nearly there."

"Nearly where?"

Kak Soran shrugged and didn't answer.

Half an hour later, the minibus stopped with a jerk.

"Out! Get out!" the interpreter said. They were the first words he'd spoken since the start of the journey. He hurried off through the door of a nearby building.

The others all humped their luggage out, and the minibus drove off. They were left standing in a huddle, their bags and bundles on the ground all round them, waiting for whatever would happen next, and looking round at the camp.

The moon was still up, and in its cold white light the place looked eerie. They seemed to be on a high bare plateau between two sheer mountain peaks. It looked like a barren, miserable place. Tara shivered. It was chilly even now, in the middle of summer. In winter it would be terrible.

They were standing outside a cluster of square

concrete buildings with a flagpole on top of the
tallest. Beyond were rows of small wooden huts
in long straight lines, which all had a door but no
window. The moonlight glinted on their
corrugated iron roofs. Tara looked back along
the road they'd come by. There didn't seem to be
any gates or fences. Perhaps they'd be allowed to
come and go as they liked. Then she noticed how
absolutely silent it was. There was nowhere to go,
from this wild, remote place. It would be madness
to try and escape from the camp. No one could
survive for long in these waterless mountains,
unless they had food and water, and knew exactly
where they were going.

Minutes ticked by. No one came and nothing
happened.

"Are they just going to leave us here all night,
without anything, without even a drink of
water?" one of the other women said suddenly.
She talked more loudly than she meant to, and
her voice seemed to boom out in the thin
mountain air.

No one had to answer because just then the
interpreter came back.

"This way," he said, starting off towards the
central two-storey building in the middle of the
concrete headquarters block. "No, not you."
Once again the door was barred to Tara who was
about to follow her father. "Only men in here.
Women in that room."

The men were away for a long time. Tara was
glad Hero was still asleep. Daya seemed more

than half asleep too. She looked hot and flushed in spite of the cold night air.

At last the interpreter came back with Kak Soran and the camp commandant, a tall, middle-aged major. All the bags and bundles were opened, and their contents tipped out on the bare concrete floor, just as they had been yesterday. Every piece of clothing, every packet of food, every pot of ointment or pair of shoes was carefully examined, just as they had been yesterday.

"Money," said the interpreter. "He wants to know how much money you've got."

Kak Soran seemed to expect the question. He put his hand inside his jacket and brought out a thin roll of notes. The major licked his thumb and counted them slowly. Then he looked hard at Kak Soran.

"No more?" said the interpreter. "Hasn't your wife got any jewellery? Anything hidden? Think carefully before you answer."

Kak Soran shook his head. Tara suddenly realized she was clasping her hands tightly together. She forced herself to let go and look unconcerned.

The major handed some of the notes back, and the rest he put in the drawer of the desk.

"He'll keep it for you," the interpreter said. "You'll get it back when you leave here."

"When will that be?" said Kak Soran quickly, sensing an opportunity.

"How should I know?" said the interpreter,

shrugging his shoulders.

Then the questions began. It was just as if the interrogations of two days ago had never happened. The major asked the same old things again and again.

"Who are you? What's your name? Why did you leave Iraq? Why did you come to Iran?"

At last Hero woke up and started grizzling. The major seemed to see her for the first time. He looked quickly at her, then at Teriska Khan, and then he began to move some papers round on his desk. He muttered something to the interpreter.

I think he's sorry for us, thought Tara with surprise. He could be a nice person.

The interpreter stood up.

"The major will see you again tomorrow," he said. "Be quick, pick your things up. I'll take you to your quarters."

They had already learned what "quick" meant. They got down on their hands and knees and began to scrabble their belongings together in desperate haste. The major said something else.

"He says to take your time," the interpreter said unwillingly.

Tara felt tears in her eyes. She wasn't expecting kindness. It made her feel weak, and painfully grateful.

Their bags were ready at last. They picked them up, and followed the interpreter, who called Kak Soran out of the next room. Then they went out into the moonlight again, and dragged all their stuff down the long rows to a cabin near the edge of the camp. Teriska Khan could hardly walk. She kept stumbling, and every now and then she coughed. The interpreter took a key out of his pocket, unlocked the cheap padlock on the door, and opened it. They went inside. Kak Soran felt for a light switch near the door, found it, and pressed it down. Nothing happened.

"The electricity in the cabins is only on in the evenings," the interpreter said.

Moonlight streamed in through the open door. The cabin was empty. Its wooden walls were stained and its floor was unswept.

"A – a carpet? Blankets?" said Teriska Khan in a hesitant voice to the interpreter, who was in a hurry to go.

"Ask tomorrow," he said. "You can get a heater and some blankets then. You'll have to make do for tonight."

He went away. Hero started crying again but for once no one took any notice of her. Tara sat down on the nearest bundle, put her arms round her knees, and began to rock herself backwards and forwards. Then, in the pale moonlight, she saw something move near her foot.

"What's that, Baba?" she said.

Kak Soran bent down to look, then squashed the insect under his foot.

"Bugs," he said. "This place is infested."

He stood up, and looked across to Teriska Khan. It was funny, thought Tara, she'd never realized it before, but even though he was a man and head of the family, of course, he always looked to Daya in a crisis, especially when the crisis was at home. But now, for the first time, he seemed to realize that she was ill. She was coughing more and more, a dry hard little cough, and she couldn't stand. She just lay down where she was on the cold hard floor and shut her eyes.

"This is awful, terrible," he said to Tara. "She can't stay here."

He seemed to crumple, as if all the strength had gone out of him.

"She's ill," he said. `

Tara was cold, hungry and exhausted, and she nearly sat down and cried like Hero. Then she felt a cold shiver of fear creep over her. There was no point in crying. No one would be able to comfort her. They were all looking to her for comfort now.

"She'll be all right, Baba," she said. "There must be a doctor here. Anyway, I'll look after her."

"You don't know how to."

"I do. I'll make sure she rests, and I'll do the cooking, and get her plenty to drink."

"But there isn't even any water."

"There's a tap, the man said, at the other end of the camp. I can go and fetch it like I did at the village. I'll find a little pot for Hero. She can help too."

The idea of Hero carrying water seemed to be the last straw. Kak Soran went to the doorway and stood staring out across the camp to the mountain peaks, which were glittering under their ghostly white caps of snow. Tara's fear turned to anger.

"We haven't got any choice," she said bitterly, repeating something one of the women had said the night before. "When you're refugees you haven't got any choice."

She unrolled a blanket and tucked it gently round her mother. Then she made a little nest of spare clothes.

"Come on, Hero," she said. "I've made a bed for you. You'll be nice and cosy here."

17

Although they were all so tired, it was just as well that night was a short one. Tara was too worried and too hungry and cold to go to sleep properly. There was hardly any bedding, certainly not enough to stop up the cracks between the floorboards and there were howling draughts everywhere.

The cold wasn't the worst thing though. Only a few minutes after she'd dropped off into a light doze, Tara woke up again, her skin crawling and itching. She sat up and scratched her arms and chest. She seemed to be covered with insects, dozens of them. She scrambled to her feet.

"Aagh!" she said. "Get off!"

"It's only a nightmare," mumbled Kak Soran, vaguely aware of a disturbance. He obviously thought Hero was dreaming again. Tara took a deep breath. A week ago she wouldn't have been able to stop herself screaming. But now the thought of disturbing the rest of the family stopped her. Hero was peaceful and quiet, and Daya seemed to be asleep. Tara could hear her shallow rasping breath. There was no point in waking them up. In the dark they wouldn't be able to do much about the bugs. She'd just have to wait till it got light, and deal with them then.

She was beginning to feel a bit steadier. She shook out her clothes one by one. It was awful to think there might still be bugs in them, but it was too cold to undress. She seemed to have got rid of most of them anyway. She felt one more, crawling across her shoulder blade, and managed to catch it and nip it between her fingers before it could bite her.

"Think of Ashti and Rostam," she told herself desperately. They were probably sleeping alongside cows and sheep, or out on the open hillsides. They'd have snakes and scorpions to worry about. The pesh murgas wouldn't let a few bedbugs bother them.

It was impossible to go to sleep after that. Tara lay down again, but she didn't relax for a minute. She was on full alert, ready to pounce on every tiny tickle.

Just before the sun came up, a wild screaming noise, coming from close by, broke the silence. Tara felt her hair stand on end. It sounded like an animal in a trap, or someone out of their mind with terror. It stopped suddenly, dying away in a horrible gobbling sound.

Almost at once another sound took its place. A loudspeaker somewhere overhead was blasting out the voice of the muezzin, calling the camp to the first prayers of the day. In spite of the crackling and distortion of the cheap amplifiers, the familiar words sounded beautiful and comforting.

"In the name of God, the Compassionate, the Merciful," the unseen mullah chanted. "I bear witness that there is no God but God, and Mohammed is his prophet."

"Compassionate and merciful," she thought. "Oh God, be compassionate and merciful now. To us."

She waited for the chant to tail away on the high, fluting note she'd always loved, but it didn't. It was suddenly cut off, and then there was a lot of deafening static that set her teeth on edge, and a confused mixture of prayers and chants, music and shouting voices that went on and on, making her want to put her hands over her ears.

For once in her life, Tara was the first of the family to get up. She crept about trying not to disturb the others, who were still lying with their eyes shut in spite of the terrible noise. As soon as the sun was touching the snowy peaks above the valley she was out of the cabin and off to the latrine, where a long line of sleepy yawning people were already waiting.

When she got back a woman was standing outside the next door cabin, shaking out a blanket. She was a large person with muscular arms and a loud voice, which was just as well because the loudspeakers were so noisy they had to practically shout to make themselves heard.

She smiled as she looked Tara up and down.

"Did you arrive last night?"

"Yes."

"A big family, are you?"

"No, there's only my parents and my little sister and me."

"That's good. You won't be too crowded. There's eight of us trying to sleep in this hutch. When one turns over we all have to."

Tara smiled back at her, wondering if all the other members of her family were as big as she was.

"Do you know – is there a doctor here?" she asked shyly. "My mother's ill."

The woman shook her head.

"No, there isn't. Not what you'd call a proper doctor, anyway. At least, I haven't heard of anyone getting any help. What's the matter?"

"I don't know. She's coughing a lot and she's got a fever."

"Hm, you'll have to look after her carefully. Are you sure you can manage?"

"Yes," said Tara uncertainly. "Where do you get food and everything?"

The woman laughed shortly.

"*You* can't go and get it. The men have to collect the rations. And precious small they are too. Did you bring anything of your own?"

"A bit I think," said Tara, trying to remember what was in the bags.

The woman hesitated, then she said abruptly,

"I've got a few things put by. I can let you have some olives and dried fruit for your mother, poor soul. She'll need food she can fancy."

"Oh, thank you!" Tara suddenly felt less alone. "The man last night said we could get blankets and a carpet today."

"Yes, of sorts. Tell your father to talk to my husband. He knows the right way to go about it. You'll need as much as you can to keep the draughts out."

"Is it always that cold at night? There were bugs too."

The woman shrugged.

"You'll just have to do the best you can with them. They're not easy to get rid of, but I've got a bit of Dettol left. I could let you have some. You'll get soap, if you could call it that, with your food ration. Give the place a good clean out, that's my advice. I'd give you a hand, but my youngest is down with the measles, and I've got my work cut out looking after him."

A fit of coughing came from the cabin and Tara turned to go.

"Good luck," the woman said. "Don't worry about your mother. She'll be all right, God willing. Make her some nice hot tea. They'll give you a paraffin stove later, but I'll let you have some hot water for now if you like. I've just boiled some up."

For the rest of the morning, Tara worked like a beaver. She scraped the skin off her knuckles scrubbing at the floor boards, and got blisters from the heavy buckets she fetched from the standpipe at the far end of the camp. But the thought of the bugs crawling and biting in the night was worse than sore hands and she plunged on, inspired by loathing for them, determined to kill them all.

"You look like Granny," Hero said, watching her curiously from the door.

"Good," said Tara, on her hands and knees, working away at a stain on the floor.

She'd hardly finished cleaning the floor when Kak Soran was back with their first lot of food rations and a tiny paraffin stove.

"Do you think you can manage?" he said doubtfully, looking down at the bags of flour, rice and tea, the handful of onions and minute cube of meat.

Tara didn't answer. She took the stuff, piled it in a corner and waited until he'd gone off to ask for blankets, then she went over to where Teriska Khan was lying, flushed and muttering, on the hard floor.

"Daya," she whispered, "are you awake?"

Teriska Khan opened her eyes but didn't seem to see her.

"Daya, how do I cook the supper? There's only a scrap of meat and no vegetables."

"Run over to Mrs Amina and ask for some eggs." Teriska Khan's voice was high and husky. "It's easy to cook eggs."

"But Daya . . ."

"Get me some water, Tara. From my dressing table. The filter . . ."

Tara straightened up. Her legs felt shaky. Daya's mind was wandering and she looked

174

terribly ill. She went to the pot of water. It was empty. She picked it up and shot out through the cabin door.

"Stay there," she said to Hero, "be a good girl. Don't bother Daya, or I'll . . ."

Hero didn't bother to look up. She'd found a little girl of her own age and they were playing together with a pile of stones.

It seemed a mile to the standpipes. She ran as fast as she could, darting between surprised looking people. But when she got to the pipes her heart sank. There was a queue of women waiting to fill their buckets.

"Please," she said desperately to the person at the front, "my mother's ill, she needs water." The woman smiled at her. She'd already filled one of her buckets and the other was standing under the trickling tap, slowly filling up.

"Here," she said, "give me your pot."

She dipped it into her full bucket and gave it to Tara.

"Don't spill it!" she called out after her, but Tara was off already, running slowly with her knees bent, her eyes fixed on the full pot, hardly spilling a drop.

The water seemed to do Teriska Khan good. She lay back after a few sips and put her head down again on Kak Soran's spare jacket that Tara had made into a kind of pillow.

If only we could turn off this awful noise, thought Tara, watching her helplessly and hating the din that bellowed endlessly from the loudspeakers.

"How's she doing then?" said a voice at the door. Tara turned, trying to control her tears. It was the woman from next door.

"I don't know," she said.

The woman came in and squatted down beside Teriska Khan.

"Listen to that breathing," she said. "It's pneumonia all right. Didn't you bring any medicine with you?"

"Just some paracetemol and a few things like that," said Tara. "Baba's given her some of that already."

The woman picked up Teriska Khan's headscarf that lay on the floor beside her.

"Dip this in the water and put it on her forehead. It'll cool her down a bit. What have you given her to eat?"

"Nothing. I haven't started to cook yet. I . . ."

The woman saw the pile of unopened rations.

"Give them to me," she said. "I'll do your dinner for you tonight. You sit with your mother, poor soul, and fan her, and keep giving her sips of water. Make sure she's warm enough. She's bad, I can see. There's a lot here with fevers. Very sudden, they come on. Lost a lot of babies and old people since we arrived. She looks strong enough, but I wouldn't like to say . . . still, you never know . . ."

She shook her head, picked up the rations and went out.

Tara sat on her heels, nursing her knees. She

wanted to run after the neighbour and shout at her, tell her she was ignorant and stupid. How dare she hint that Daya was in danger? What did she know about it anyway? Daya had only started being ill two days ago. People couldn't die as quickly as that, surely?

She poured a little water onto the scarf and laid it gently on Teriska Khan's forehead. Then she touched her hand. It felt very hot and dry. She took the scarf off her head and gently sponged her hands with it.

"Compassionate and Merciful," she said to herself. "Compassionate and Merciful. Don't die. Don't die."

The next two days and nights were like a nightmare that went on and on. The little cabin was filled with the dreadful rasping sound of Teriska Khan's breathing, punctuated by her painful cough. Kak Soran and Tara were already exhausted from their journey but they didn't have much chance to rest. Kak Soran had to spend hours at the camp headquarters, being questioned. The fact that his wife was ill didn't cut any ice with anyone there. The rest of the time he had to spend queuing for rations, and trying to get hold of carpets and blankets.

When he did come back to the cabin his face showed how tense and anxious he felt, but he didn't seem to know what to do. He'd never nursed a sick person before. Tara hadn't either. Half the time she felt so frightened she wanted to do nothing but scream and scream. Then her feelings would change to a boiling rage.

"You're not going to die!" she'd mutter through clenched teeth. "I'm not going to let you."

She sat beside Teriska Khan all day, watching her like a hawk, while the kind neighbour fetched the water she needed and cooked their meals.

At every slight movement or change Tara would be on the alert at once, trying to work out what it might mean, how Daya felt and how she could be made more comfortable. When her breathing got very loud and heavy, her lips became dry and cracked. Tara would feed her spoonfuls of water to moisten them. If Daya started moaning and thrashing, Tara would see she was burning with fever, and she'd grind up a paracetemol tablet and slip it into her mouth with some water, and wash her face and hands. She spent hours fanning her, and trying to make the primitive bedclothes more comfortable. She talked to her, on and on, whether Teriska Khan seemed to be able to hear or not. She told her to get better, and scolded her for being too hot. Sometimes she cried, and pleaded with her not to die, and prayed, and coaxed her to drink a little soup or a mouthful of tea.

At night, Tara sank into a few hours of exhausted sleep herself, but she was on guard and ready to jump up at once if she was needed. Kak Soran hardly slept at all, but sat beside his wife, watching for any sign of a change, and settling Hero if she woke up. At least, thought Tara thankfully, she didn't have to worry about Hero. The little girl she'd found to play with had become her friend, and Yasmin's mother kindly offered to look after Hero until the crisis was over. Hero asked once or twice why Daya wasn't getting up, but with so many other changes in her life, Teriska Khan's strange behaviour didn't seem as peculiar as it would have done at home.

At dawn on the third morning, Tara was woken as usual by the brutal assault of the loudspeakers, and she sat up at once, guiltily aware that she'd slept for longer than she'd meant to. In the cracks of light that came in through the badly fitting door she could see the shapes of her parents, two motionless bundles on the floor. She couldn't hear Daya breathing at all.

She shut her eyes tight for a moment, desperately afraid. When she opened them again Kak Soran was unrolling himself from his blanket. He sat up, and in the dim light Tara could see he was smiling at her.

"Asleep," he said quietly. "The fever's gone."

There was a knock at the door. Tara scrambled over to open it. The neighbour's big husband stood outside.

"How is the lady?" he said, looking very solemn.

"Sleeping! Better!" said Tara, wiping the tears from her streaked face with the end of her long sleeve.

Kak Soran came to the door.

"Slept well for a good four hours," he said,

"and no fever this morning."

The man took his hand and pumped it up and down.

"And my wife was afraid to come and ask herself!" he said, grinning from ear to ear. "She thought last night . . . She will be pleased! And she's bringing some tea and a mouthful of breakfast round for you all."

18

Teriska Khan didn't get better all at once. She was as weak as a kitten for days. At first even trying to sit up tired her out. She had almost no appetite and lay listlessly, all day long, staring out of the open door. Tara longed to be able to give her little pieces of fresh fruit, or sweet things like honey cakes, anything tasty that would tempt her to eat, but there was nothing but the dullest, plainest food. Anyway she thought, seeing the look in her eyes, Teriska Khan probably didn't even notice what she was eating. She was thinking all the time about Ashti and Granny and home.

"You'll have to be careful now," the neighbour said, when she'd got Tara out of earshot. "Your mother could relapse and she wouldn't come through so easily a second time. She needs to build up her strength. Try and cheer her up and get her to eat. I'd do more for you if I could but my second's gone down with the measles too, and he looks really bad. I hope you and the little girl have had it?"

"Yes, we have," said Tara thankfully. Measles on top of everything else would be the last straw.

For the next few weeks Tara worked harder than she'd ever worked in her life. The whole family depended on her. She couldn't rely on the neighbour any more. She had to be up first, and prepare the samovar for the morning tea. She had to get breakfast for Baba and Hero, and persuade Daya to eat a little bread, and fetch water for Daya to wash in, and pick over the rice to get the grit out of it before she could cook it for supper.

She looked after Hero too. She did everything for her, took her to the latrines, got her meals ready, helped her to wash and get dressed and cuddled her when she was tired or cross. It was funny but the more she had to do for Hero the better she got on with her. It wasn't the same as just helping Daya look after her. It was quite different now she was in charge herself and had to think of everything on her own. Hero could be really difficult sometimes, especially when she didn't get her own way, but Tara seemed able to manage her more easily.

The biggest battle of all was against the bugs. Tara scoured the cabin from floor to ceiling using a few drops of the precious Dettol in each bucket of water. She scrubbed and rubbed at the filthy blankets they'd been given, and beat clouds of dust and muck out of the thin strip of carpet until her arms ached.

Then she washed her hair and Hero's hair again and again in the hard, coarse soap they were issued with, and Teriska Khan carefully inspected it in case they'd caught lice. The soap made their hair smell unpleasant, and it felt lank and heavy. Tara's scalp itched too.

If ever I get to use proper shampoo again, she thought longingly, I'll know just how wonderful it is.

This great burst of activity required huge quantities of water and Tara went backwards and forwards time after time to the standpipes. She soon got fed up with standing in a long queue, then staggering back with a full bucket, which always slopped into her shoes. It was so difficult to hold the sides of the wretched chador tightly together under her chin with her spare hand.

By the end of the first week the cabin was habitable. The walls and floor were spotless and the carpet even gave it a furnished look. After all the beatings and scrubbings Tara had given it, it looked more ragged and threadbare than ever, but at least it was clean. Tara hadn't quite got rid of the revolting smell that still clung to the blankets, but they were much better than they had been. It was a rare bug now that dared invade the cabin, and everyone began sleeping properly again.

Tara was no longer woken by the screams and yells that still broke out every night. They weren't nearly so frightening now she knew where they were coming from. It was a poor man, the friendly neighbour's husband had told Kak Soran, who had lost his wife and three small children in a bombing raid. His brother had managed to get him through the mountains to the refugee camp, but now he'd started having fits, and no one could do anything with him till he'd calmed down.

As the weeks passed, Teriska Khan grew stronger. She began to potter about the cabin and take over the cooking. She supervised the washing and did more and more for Hero. But even though things seemed to be getting back to normal again it wasn't the same as it had been before she'd been ill. Tara didn't need telling now when things needed to be done. She'd pick up the bucket and go off for water before anyone else noticed it was empty. She'd fold up the blankets and stack them neatly away as soon as everyone was up. She'd take the rations out of Kak Soran's hands and arrange them in the little store area she'd planned out while Teriska Khan was ill.

She and Daya talked about different things now too. There was no question any more of hiding things from Tara, as if she was still a little girl. For the first time she asked questions, and Daya talked freely, as if Tara had been Auntie Suzan or someone. Tara began to understand things that had always vaguely puzzled her in the past. It was like fitting together the pieces of a broken jug. Things that Baba had let fall, Rostam's stories, the piece of paper the boys outside the mosque had been reading, the unexplained disappearances of friends' fathers and brothers, the arrests and beatings, the propaganda and terror all added up to a new idea of what it meant to be a Kurd, and she felt proud and angry at the same time.

Once all the washing and scrubbing was done there seemed to be nothing to do except talk, and time passed very slowly. During the day Kak Soran wasn't around much. Sometimes he was summoned to the camp headquarters for further questioning, or was made to watch propaganda videos on the victory Iran would soon have over Iraq. Usually he spent whatever time he had left over in deep conversation with the other men in the camp, who came to him for advice, or to ask his opinion of the latest rumours that seemed to arrive from nowhere. As soon as he showed his face at the cabin door, Teriska Khan would question him. Was there any news? Had he been able to contact anyone, get a letter off to Teheran? When would they be able to get out of here and start leading a civilised life again?

It was a while before the truth dawned on them all. There was no chance of getting out. They wouldn't be allowed to write letters, or make telephone calls, or leave the camp at all, under any pretext. Anyway, Kak Soran's friends in Teheran were Kurds too. They were probably trying to keep themselves out of trouble. It would be dangerous for them to be in touch with enemy aliens, as all Iraqi Kurds in Iran now were.

Once she stopped hoping to get out of the camp, Tara began to lose track of time. She'd been keyed up with euphoria and relief when Daya had got better, but that had all gone now. She started feeling low and depressed. There were other girls of her age at the camp, but she couldn't be bothered to get really friendly with them. It was easier just to be alone or spend her time with Daya. Teriska Khan wasn't ill any more now, but she hadn't ever quite got back to being her old self again. Tara still did more of her share of household chores, but when the odd jobs were all done, she'd spend hours doing nothing, just sitting and staring into space.

"If only I'd brought some vitamin pills," said Teriska Khan looking at her worriedly. "This awful diet's no good for growing children."

Late summer changed into autumn. The snow on the summits began to creep slowly down the mountainside. One morning the refugees woke to find a light dusting of it on the ground all round them. Teriska Khan groaned when she saw it.

"Look at them! Look at them!" she said, holding out a protesting Hero's feet towards her husband. "Do you see these shoes? Two sizes too small! She can't possibly wear them any longer, even though I've cut out the toes and heels. And how is she to go outside without them in this weather, I'd like to know?"

Hero's shoes really upset Kak Soran. He couldn't bear the thought of her going out with bare feet in the snow. The next day he went to the camp HQ and begged them to get hold of a pair of shoes for her. The man in the office shrugged, and said it was impossible. They weren't allowed to supply anything that wasn't listed in the document he waved in Kak Soran's face. Kak

Soran put his hand into his sash as if he was going to get out some money, and offered to pay whatever they asked. The man shrugged again. Kak Soran began to raise his voice and lose his temper, but luckily, a friendly fellow refugee was in the office at the time, waiting to see the authorities himself. He took Kak Soran by the arm and almost dragged him out of the camp office.

"You must keep calm," the man said to him earnestly outside. "They could flog you, or cut your rations, or lock you up in the prison house if you offend them. Look, there's a family near my cabin with a child a year or two older than your little girl. Perhaps they've got some shoes he's grown out of."

Kak Soran followed him gratefully. The man's neighbours didn't have any shoes to spare, but he wouldn't give up. He went up and down the lines of cabins, looking out for children a bit larger than Hero who might have grown out of their shoes. He came home at last, with a pair of broken sandals in his hand.

"It's the best I could do," he said. "You'll have to sew the strap on again. Tell Hero to look after them. They cost me a small fortune."

Tara was growing too, in spite of the bad diet. Though all she had to eat was small amounts of rice and bread, with an occasional helping of meat and vegetables, her trousers had had to be let down, and the sleeves of her sweaters were too short at the wrists. She hadn't seen a mirror for months. She had no idea what she looked like any more.

"Perhaps we'll be here for ever," she thought, looking at her bare wrists in horror. "Perhaps I'll grow old here, and never get out, and never have any other life at all."

19

Autumn, 1984

"It's mine!"

"No, it's mine!"

"My granny gave it to me!"

"She didn't. My auntie gave it to me!"

Hero stamped her foot.

"I hate you! You're horrible, and nasty, and —
and you smell!"

Yasmin burst into tears.

"You're not my friend any more, and you can't
play with my dolly, and . . ."

Teriska Khan, looking pale and exhausted, was
talking to Yasmin's mother. They were sitting
close to the paraffin stove, leaning against the
cabin wall, deep in conversation. They obviously
didn't want to be disturbed.

"Tara," said Teriska Khan, "can't you do
something with them? Play a game, or give them
some sugar, or something."

At the magic word, the crying stopped. The
two little girls dropped the scrap of shawl they'd
been fighting over and rushed up to Tara, pulling
at her clothes to make her stand up.

"Stop it," said Tara irritably, getting to her

feet.

She was fed up with giving sugar to Hero. The family's weekly ration was tiny and Teriska Khan hoarded it carefully in an old tin which Kak Soran had salvaged from the back of the storehouse. Tara hardly ever got any of it. Most of it was saved for the tea that Teriska Khan liked to offer fellow refugees who dropped in at the cabin. One way or another, Hero usually got all the rest.

Tara lifted the tin down from its high shelf and scooped a few white grains into each grubby hand. Hero licked hers up quickly.

"More," she said, holding her hand out again.

"More," said Yasmin, copying her.

"Only if you promise not to fight," said Tara. Hero and Yasmin nodded. They looked so serious and greedy that Tara couldn't help laughing. She gave them each another little pinch.

"That's all," she said, putting the tin back on its shelf. "Now why don't you play with rabbit?"

Hero and Yasmin looked at each other, wondering whether or not to go on quarrelling. Then a dazzling smile broke over Hero's face, and she flung her arm round Yasmin's neck.

"My Rabbit got blowed up in a bomb," she said, "and his house fell down, and he ran away on a horse in the middle of the night, and now we've got to make him a nice bed and give him something to eat."

Tara sighed with relief. They'd be happily occupied for a while, until the next quarrel flared up anyway, and she could go back to – go back to

190

what? What had she been doing before Daya had called her? Nothing. She could go back to doing nothing. She sat down again, and rested her back against the rough wooden wall of the cabin.

"Did you hear all that noise last night?" said Yasmin's mother. "I didn't get a wink of sleep. Trucks and buses coming and going, and soldiers shouting, and some woman crying and crying . . ."

"We don't hear much down this end," said Teriska Khan. "You're near the main buildings, aren't you? It's quieter here."

"There was a big crowd of new arrivals. Twenty at least, I should think. I don't know where they'll put them all."

"Did you hear where they come from? Was there anyone we know? Perhaps they'll have some news."

"I'm not sure. There were a couple of families from Sulaimaniya, but most of them came from the villages. I didn't hear them mention any village names though."

Teriska Khan shivered.

"Poor things, coming over at this time of year. It was bad enough in the summer, but the mountain passes must be all snowed up by now."

"Yes. Apperently it's terrible. I heard such a sad story from one of them. There was an old man with a bad leg, and . . ."

Tara stood up and reached for her chador. She couldn't face any more sad stories today. She'd heard enough of them to last a lifetime.

"I've got to go to the toilet," she said, and opened the door. The blast of cold wind made her shiver. She hurried down the line of cabins towards the latrine, hoping there wouldn't be a queue of people waiting. She'd freeze if she had to stand around in this wind for long.

Luckily there was no one waiting. She screwed her nose up against the awful smell, did what she had to do, and rushed out of the latrine as quickly as she could. Then, near the standpipe, where a group of women were talking, she heard a familiar name.

"Yes, it's like I told you. My son's been with Kak Rostam. He came through last night, with about five or six other pesh murgas. One of them was badly hurt. I don't know about the others. You should see my son's face! Scars all over it, and as for his arms . . ."

Tara pushed through the group of black veiled women.

"Excuse me," she said. "Did you say that some of Kak Rostam's men are here? You don't know if – there isn't one called Ashti Hawrami, is there? He's my brother."

The woman pursed her lips, trying to remember.

"No, I don't think so. Hawrami . . . he isn't related to Kak Rostam, is he?"

"Yes. His nephew."

Her forehead cleared.

"Oh, I remember now. My son's been talking about him. Ashti – yes, that was the name.

Injured his shoulder, didn't he? Apparently that hasn't stopped him. He led my son on a raid last week. A real daredevil, Bakir says, though he's only a boy and looks the studious type."

Tara felt suddenly lighter, as if she'd had a weight pressing down on her head and it had rolled off. She almost felt she could fly.

"Oh, thank you, thank you!" she said. "Where's your cabin? I must go and tell Baba and Daya. They'll want to come and talk to your son. Oh, I can't believe it! You don't know how much . . ."

She almost burst into tears. The woman smiled kindly and patted her on the shoulder.

"Of course I know," she said. "I hadn't heard from my son for months. My cabin's in that row there, third from the end. Tell your Daya she can come and see me any time she likes and I'll tell Bakir, Kak Ashti's father'll be paying him a visit. He'll be pleased. He thinks a lot of your brother."

Looking back later, Tara felt that everything changed after the news of Ashti came. Bakir and his friends seemed to have brought good luck with them. Things had been getting worse for months, ever since Rostam had arrived in Sulaimaniya that evening, that seemed so long ago. From now on everything started, very slowly, to get better.

The first sign came the next day when Kak Soran came back to the cabin with the weekly ration of rice and flour. He put it down on the floor beside the paraffin stove, where Teriska

Khan was stirring a pot of lentils. Both of them had been much more cheerful since they'd talked to Bakir and had heard first hand that Ashti was alive and well, and that his shoulder seemed to have mended nicely.

"Things are beginning to happen," said Kak Soran in a voice that sounded livelier than it had done for a long time. "They're moving people on. Three families left last night, and they all arrived here at the same time as us, or a little earlier. I've got a feeling we won't be here much longer."

Tara didn't dare even to think about it. The idea of leaving was too unsettling. If she started to hope, and then was disappointed, she'd get so depressed she couldn't imagine what she'd do. At the same time, although she wanted more than anything else to leave this horrible place, she was frightened. Perhaps they'd be taken somewhere even worse. They might be separated, or sent back to face the bombing again, or locked up, or beaten, or . . . She tried not to think about it.

But when they were finally sent for, she realized she'd been waiting for this moment all the time. It was just getting dark. The floodlights had been switched on, and they were glaring down from the tall masts that towered over the rows of the cabins. The camp was quietening down to its evening routine. The men were coming out from the room in the main building where prayers had finished a while ago. The women were dishing out the evening meal to their waiting families, or standing at their cabin doors, chatting to neighbours.

Tara was on her way back from the standpipes with a bucket of water for the family's nightly wash. She'd almost arrived at the cabin when the deafening crackle of music from the loudspeakers overhead was cut off. There was a pause, a burst of static, and then a voice barked out:

"The following families are to be transferred. They will report in one hour to the main building. Dilshad Zehn, Shawan Mosuli . . ."

The voice droned on. Tara got to the cabin door, and put down her bucket on a flat stone that Kak Soran had put there to stop the ground getting too muddy. Then she bent down to take off her shoes before she went inside.

"Soran Hawrami, Teriska Hawrami, Tara Hawrami, Hero Hawrami . . ."

She raced inside.

"Daya! Didn't you hear? They called out our names! We're being transferred! We've got to be ready in an hour!"

Teriska Khan looked up from the darn she was finishing in Kak Soran's sock.

"What? I didn't hear anything. What are you talking about?"

Kak Soran rushed in through the door, pushing Tara out of the way.

"It's true. Come on. We've got to get packed up at once."

"But . . ."

"No time for questions. Quick. Get out the bags. Roll up the bedding. Tara, get these clothes

195

into some order. And Teriska, sort out these cooking things. No, of course you can't go and say goodbye to Yasmin's mother. Send a message if you like. She'll come and wave us goodbye. Now, for goodness sake, get a move on. If we're not ready and waiting by eight o'clock they'll simply leave us behind."

The next hour was like living through a speeded up film. After so many months of doing nothing, and making up things to do to make the endless hours go faster, every second was suddenly precious. They worked so hard they'd got everything rolled up and packed in fifty minutes, and a crowd of friendly neighbours helped them take all their bags and bundles down the long line of cabins to the waiting minibuses.

Tara almost felt a lump in her throat. People were being so kind, especially to Teriska Khan, whose illness and recovery had made news in the camp. She looked round at the circle of friendly Kurdish faces. Perhaps if she hadn't been so homesick and so depressed all the time she'd have got to know some of them a bit better. As it was, the only people she was really sorry to say goodbye to were the neighbour and her husband, who'd done what they could to help when Daya had been so ill. She hadn't got to know them very well, but she still felt she was leaving her only friends behind.

A jeep full of soldiers drove up to the head of the little convoy, and Tara saw the major who'd checked them in on their first evening get out of it. He got them to file past him into the minibuses and as they went he put ticks against their names on the list he held in his hand. Then he jumped back into the front seat of the jeep and the drivers of the two minibuses full of refugees started up their engines and swung round the first corner behind him. Their headlights swept round and lit up the crowd of tattered refugees left behind, then picked up in their strong beams the rocks that lined the road. They began the slow winding journey down the mountainside.

"Why don't they ever *tell* us anything?" Tara whispered to Kak Soran. "Why do they always make us go at night? We don't even know where we've been all this time, or where they're taking us now."

Four months ago she wouldn't have expected a real answer, but since Teriska Khan had been ill he'd got into the habit of talking to her more seriously.

"I suppose they've got their reasons," he said at last. "Military reasons. What matters is that we mustn't show we're frightened or angry. We've got to try and stay in control, and not give up hope. It's not as if we're alone, after all. There are twenty million Kurds. They can't keep us down for ever."

That's not much of an answer, thought Tara crossly, but she didn't dare say anything out loud.

"Why can't we just live in peace?" she said. "Why doesn't everyone leave us alone?"

This time, Kak Soran didn't answer.

20

Tara sat under a tree sewing. The hem of her skirt was so ragged it hardly seemed worth trying to patch it. She broke off the short end of cotton, and threaded some more through the needle. The ripped waistband would be quite tricky to mend.

When they'd arrived at this new camp the searches had been really tough at first. Everyone, even Hero, had been stripped and gone over from head to toe. They'd started examining each bit of clothing, and some things, like the waistband on the skirt, had even been ripped open.

The searchers had pounced triumphantly on a few banknotes and a thin gold bangle, hidden in the lining of Hero's jacket. At that point Teriska Khan had gone off into a convincing show of hysterics.

"My last penny has been taken from me!" she wailed. "What is this poor woman to do, with nothing left to me but my children?"

She'd sounded so sincere and so miserable that the searchers had obviously believed that they'd found everything and had slackened off after that.

The thing they'd looked at most carefully was

the precious belt. A suspicious guard had examined it, his eyes on Teriska Khan's face. He'd felt all along it, fingered the seams and bounced it in his hands to see how heavy it was. Tara had tensed up and held her breath, but Teriska Khan seemed quite relaxed. When it was all over, Tara said,

"Why didn't they find your jewellery?"

"I moved it," said Teriska Khan complacently. "Too many people knew about it in the last camp. I guessed a whisper might have been passed on."

"Where is it now?"

"I don't think I'd better tell you. Now you get on with that pile of mending. I'm going to take Hero off for a bath."

It was amazing, thought Tara, stretching comfortably, what a difference a good bath made to how you felt about life. The showers here were the simplest you could imagine, in the barest possible room, where five people had to wash at the same time. But at least they had hot water, and really worked.

She'd nearly cried with joy when Kak Soran had come back to their funny little room in the old mud brick building yesterday with a cake of proper soap, that lathered and smelled nice, and best of all, a bottle of shampoo. She still couldn't get used to the bliss of having clean, fresh smelling hair.

She looked round the camp. It was a poor place, rough and dirty, but much, much nicer here than the camp in the mountains. The buildings hadn't been hastily knocked together out of flimsy materials specially to house unwelcome refugees. They were old, solid and square, and had perhaps been used as storehouses or stables years and years ago. Each little room, with its thick whitewashed walls and round domed roof was joined to the ones on either side, and had a heavy wooden door leading out into the open. Trees were dotted round the camp, figs, almonds and sycamore. Their leaves were beginning to dry and turn yellow, and rattle in the breeze as autumn, which was well on in the mountains, crept day by day closer to the plain.

The weather was better here too. It was still quite mild most of the time. The snow wouldn't come for a month or so yet. The wind was a playful breeze instead of the chilling blast she'd hated so much in the mountains. It carried the familiar smells of the countryside, cows, and hay, and sunbaked earth.

That was another wonderful thing, thought Tara. Even though a high wall of brieze blocks surrounded the camp, preventing them from seeing anything of the outside world, she had a clear idea of where they were and what lay beyond. They'd arrived in daylight, in the early morning, driving across the open, pleasant countryside of Iran. They'd seen villages, and the patchwork of fields, yellow and brown after the harvest. Best of all, Teheran was only an hour's drive away. Kak Soran had already got hold of a pass and had gone in to the city to start the search for the few friends and relations he hoped were still living there. He was talking optimistically about his papers, and about applying for work permits.

Perhaps, thought Tara, perhaps we might . . .

The thread snapped in her fingers. It was just as well, she thought, looking down at it. Like a vine shooting out its little tendrils, small feelers of hope kept sprouting in her mind, hope for a proper home, for a settled place, for school and friends. But she mustn't hope for anything. Not yet.

"Tara! Tara!"

She turned. Hero was skipping towards her, her hair still wet from the shower.

"Smell me, Tara. I'm all nice now. Smell me here, and here, and here."

Tara put her sewing down, picked Hero up and put her on her knee. Hero did smell lovely. She buried her face in Hero's neck. It tickled. Hero wriggled and giggled. She was happy and excited.

"Take your scarf off," she said bossily. "I want to smell your hair."

"No, I mustn't," said Tara regretfully. The worst thing here was the regulation clothing. The women all had to wear a navy scarf and a grey floor length coat, with buttons running all the way down the front, over their own clothes. They were as unlike the glittering, brilliant dresses that Kurdish women all wore at home as they could possibly be. Everyone grumbled, but nobody dared to break the rules. Things might be easier here than in the other place, but one step out of line and the authorities were quick to show they meant business. It didn't do to get on the wrong side of them.

"You must take it off, you must!" said Hero. "I *want* you too!" She tugged at the front fold of the scarf, which was pulled down modestly low over Tara's forehead, to hide every stray tendril of hair.

"Hey! Don't do that! You'll get me into trouble!" said Tara, ducking her head. She was too slow. Hero quickly whisked the scarf off, and Tara's mass of dark, curly hair, soft and springy from its fresh shampooing, rolled down over her shoulders.

Hero wriggled quickly out of her lap and danced off, waving the scarf triumphantly.

"I've got it! I've got it! You can't catch me!" she chanted. She'd often played chase and catch with Yasmin at the other camp. It was one of her favourite games.

Tara scrambled to her feet.

"Come here, come back at once!" she shouted. "It's not a game! Don't you dare run away with it! Quick! Bring it back!"

She darted towards Hero, but her long straight skirt got in the way, and she nearly fell.

"Can't catch me!" said Hero, laughing at her.

"Hero! Please – give it back!" said Tara desperately, her heart thumping with fright. "You don't understand. If anyone sees me – !"

"I've got it, I've got it," said Hero in a sing-song voice, backing away from her.

Tara heard men's voices coming round the

corner of the nearest row of buildings, and she turned to run away and hide, trying to gather up her hair in her hands. It was hopeless. There was too much of it.

Then, to her relief, Kak Soran appeared, alone.

"Tara!" he said frowning at her. "Where's your scarf? You must be more careful. You've got to wear it all the time, you know that. If you're caught without it I don't know what they'll do."

"Hero snatched it off me," said Tara indignantly. "She won't give it back. Honestly, Baba, she's the limit!"

Kak Soran turned round and saw Hero smiling naughtily at him from behind the tree.

"I see," he said.

Tara waited for the smile that usually crossed Baba's face when he dealt with Hero. For once, it didn't come.

"Give Tara her scarf," he said.

Hero whipped the scarf out of sight behind her back, and dodged further behind the tree. Feeling safe there, she peeped round the trunk at him.

"No," she said experimentally.

"Hero," said Kak Soran, "give Tara her scarf back *at once*, or I'll . . ."

He didn't have to say any more. Hero didn't often hear him talk in that tone of voice but she knew quite well what it meant. She stamped forward, shaking her head crossly so that the wet curls flicked backwards and forwards over her cheeks, and dropped the square of navy blue material at Tara's feet. Tara picked it up and tied it over her hair, her fingers shaking with relief.

"You must never, never –" began Kak Soran, shaking his forefinger at Hero, but he didn't have a chance to finish.

"Soran!" someone called. He turned round. Teriska Khan, her long grey dress almost tripping her up, was hurrying towards him, her towel flapping over her arm.

"Oh, be quick," she panted. "I've just heard they're calling for you. You've got a visitor! He's waiting at the main building, over by the gate. I'm sure it's your cousin from Teheran! I hope to God it is!"

It seemed to Tara that Kak Soran was away for hours, but it was only three-quarters of an hour later when he came back. She and Teriska Khan spent the whole time watching out for him, and when he finally appeared they could see even from a distance that he looked happy. His back was straighter and he walked quickly, without the slightly drooping shuffle he'd had recently.

"Well," he said, smiling broadly. "You were quite right. It was Daban. He's a good fellow. I liked him at once. A proper family man. He says he'll do all he can to help us. He talked about my parents so respectfully, and said how kind Father was to him years ago when he was a student and his own father died."

Hero had been watching him nervously from the other side of the room. She followed his every movement as he settled himself cross-legged on the thin piece of carpet and stretched out his hand for the glass of tea that Teriska Khan had poured for him. She approached warily, then making up her mind suddenly, plumped herself down on his lap.

"Hey! Careful!" he said, holding his tea out of reach. Then he began automatically to stroke her head, hardly realising she was there, while he went on talking to Teriska Khan. Hero snuggled into the crook of his arm and shot a cunning look at Tara. He'd obviously forgotten she'd been naughty.

Tara didn't even notice her. She didn't want to miss a word.

"Yes, tomorrow, I told you. I've got passes for all of us. We can go out about nine in the morning, and we don't have to be back in the camp till six o'clock. Daban's going to pick us up in his car and take us to his house in Teheran. He says he's got a really good place there, in a nice district. I should think he's done well for himself in the last ten years."

"What's his wife called?" Teriska Khan said, thoughtfully stirring sugar into another glass of tea. In this camp, you could buy extra supplies of everything, and the whole family were still enjoying the luxury of having as much sugar as they liked in their tea.

"Noor, I think," said Kak Soran. "I haven't seen her since the wedding, years and years ago, but she comes from a village not far from ours. They got married several years before we did. There are a couple of older boys, and a daughter of Tara's age, I think, and one or two younger children. Daban says she'll be happy to take you and the girls shopping in Teheran, if you like. Then we'll have a meal with them, and they'll bring us back here in the evening."

Teriska Khan had jumped up long before he'd finished talking, and was ferreting round in one of the worn, shabby bags that lined the wall.

"My goodness," she said nervously, "going out to visit, and cousins of yours that I've never met! I don't know – I've got nothing to wear! Whatever will they think of us? We all look like . . ."

Kak Soran lifted Hero off his lap and stood up.

"Don't be silly," he said laughing. "They know what we've been through. And anyway, you can buy some new things. We've got enough money for that."

They smiled at each other triumphantly.

"And the best thing is," said Kak Soran, shooting back his cuff to look at his watch as he used to in the old days, when time was something precious, "Daban has promised to help me with my papers. He knows the ropes, how to get things sorted out. I haven't had a chance to discuss it with him yet, but I wouldn't be surprised if we're out of here and in our own home in Teheran, and the girls settled back into school before the end of the year."

Tara shivered and Teriska Khan spoke for them both.

"Oh, don't say it," she said. "Don't tempt fate. It's too dangerous to say things like that – yet."

21

"Who the hell do you think you are?" yelled Uncle Daban, leaning out of the window of his car and making a rude gesture to the driver of a taxi, who was cruising slowly along near the kerb in search of customers and holding up all the traffic behind him.

Tara was sitting in the back seat with Hero and Teriska Khan. She shut her eyes and breathed deeply. It seemed like years and years since she'd been in a busy city street, and she felt quite shaken up and scared. Baghdad in the rush hour had been pretty awful, but surely it had never been as bad as this! The traffic in Teheran was chaotic, and everyone went so fast! Cars, buses, trucks, bicycles and taxis all seemed to hurtle towards each other in a terrible free for all, horns blaring, tyres screeching, drivers cursing.

Nervously she opened her eyes and looked out of the window. What a huge city this was! She'd forgotten the feeling of being in a crowded street full of shops and tall buildings and street sellers. She'd forgotten what ordinary people looked like, people who lived in ordinary houses, doing ordinary things, leading ordinary lives. She felt as if she'd been in prison, and was seeing the world again for the first time after years of being locked away. Now she knew what it must be like to be a country person, coming for the first time from a village to the big city.

The car slowed down at a set of traffic lights. A fruit and vegetable stall was set out. Tara had almost forgotten what carrots and cabbages and onions looked like. She couldn't take her eyes off the huge scarlet tomatoes, that looked so swollen they might burst. She could just imagine herself biting into one, and feel the juice running down her chin. Next to the tomatoes was a heap of cos lettuces, with drops of dew still glistening on their crinkly leaves. Behind them were piles of grapes. Never, never, thought Tara, would she thoughtlessly munch her way through a bunch of grapes again. For the first time she realized how beautiful they were, each pearly green globe dusted with a frosty white bloom just asking to be picked gently from its bunch and delicately eaten.

Hero had been watching a crowd of schoolchildren walk past on the opposite pavement. She turned just as the lights were changing and saw the fruit stall.

"I want some grapes, I want some grapes," she started to chant, bouncing up and down on Teriska Khan's knee.

"Yes, later, be quiet now," Teriska Khan whispered.

"No, now! I want some now!" said Hero

loudly.

Uncle Daban laughed over his shoulder.

"Wait till you see what your Auntie Noor's got for you. You'll get more than grapes, I can tell you!"

The car drew up outside a high modern building.

"Here we are," said Uncle Daban, smiling broadly. They got out and stood on the pavement while Uncle Daban locked up his car. Tara looked up and down the street. She had a sudden feeling of panic. There were no walls or guards here. She could walk down this street, and no one would stop her. No one would even notice her because in a strange way the chador made you invisible. For a moment she wanted to bolt, she didn't know where to.

"Come on, let's go up," Uncle Daban said, enthusiastically making for the entrance to the building. He wasn't a bit like Baba, Tara thought, smiling at him. Kak Soran was tall and dignified. Uncle Daban was short and a bit overweight, and by the time he'd taken them up the two flights of stairs to the front door of his flat, he was puffing, and beads of sweat were starting out on his balding head.

Several hours later, Tara was leaning back against an embroidered cushion, feeling too stuffed to move. All around, on the cloth spread over the silk rug, lay the wreckage of Auntie Noor's hospitality.

I'll never forget this meal, thought Tara. It was the most wonderful I've ever had in my whole life. I'd forgotten what real food tasted like.

They seemed to have been eating for ever. The men had been served first, then they'd hurried off to meet a business contact of Uncle Daban, who had useful friends in official places. After that the rest of them had settled down to it, and now the great dish of spicy stewed lamb, the plump pieces of chicken, the bowls of fresh yoghurt and crunchy salads had almost been cleaned out. Only the big tray of pilau rice, studded with pine kernels, still seemed hardly dented.

"Almaz," said Auntie Noor to her daugher, "Give Tara another honey cake. " Almaz leant over and tried to slide one onto Tara's plate.

"I couldn't, really, I've never eaten so much in my life. It was fantastic," said Tara, feebly waving the plateful of cakes away.

"Go and show Tara your things then, darling," said Auntie Noor in a firm voice. Tara knew what that meant. She and Teriska Khan wanted to have a good talk without the girls overhearing.

Almaz stood up and smiled at Tara uncertainly.

"Oh, yes – thank you," said Tara. She struggled to her feet. Perhaps she shouldn't have had that last helping of lamb. She was feeling a bit too full. After such a long time on bad, plain food, Auntie Noor's cooking seemed almost too rich.

She followed Almaz into the bedroom she shared with her sisters. It was a small room, and the three beds took up much of the floor space. The window was covered with criss-crossed bands of sticky tape.

"That's in case of air-raids," said Almaz, following the direction of Tara's eyes. "It stops the glass shattering. There've been a lot of air-raids. It's so awful when you hear the explosions. Thank goodness we haven't had any round here. I just die when I hear the sirens go off. I'm too sensitive, really, Daya says."

Tara didn't answer. At home in Sulaimaniya every window in every house had been taped since the first week of the war.

"Do you like the curtains?" said Almaz, trying to think of something to say. "They're new. We only got them this year."

"Yes, they're lovely," said Tara, sitting down on the lilac bedspread. She looked round, desperately trying to think of something to say. She'd been looking forward so much to meeting Almaz, a cousin of her own age, someone she could really talk to and make friends with. She'd imagined herself doing things with Almaz just like she used to with Leila and her other friends. It would be like the good old days at home again. They'd be able to gossip and giggle and talk about their parents and schoolfriends.

But now she was here in Almaz's bedroom she couldn't say a word. Uncle Daban's flat was nice, though their own house in Sulaimaniya had been much bigger and grander, and the girls' bedroom wasn't half as pretty as her room at home had been. None of that mattered now. What mattered was that at six o'clock that evening she'd have to go back to the bare whitewashed cowshed where her few ragged possessions were packed in one torn bag. She was an outsider now, looking in.

"What's it like in the camp?" said Almaz curiously.

"This one isn't as bad as the first one," said Tara. "At least there are showers, and not so many bedbugs."

Almaz gave a little scream.

"Bedbugs! You're kidding! Oh, I couldn't stand that. I'm funny about insects. I just go mad if I see a spider even. I'd die if I saw a bedbug. Daya says . . ."

"You haven't got any choice in a refugee camp." Tara tried not to sound impatient. "Bedbugs aren't so bad. There are worse things than that."

"Oh, really? Yes, I suppose . . ."

Tara turned her head to gaze out of the window. Why couldn't she talk about clothes and make-up and parties any more? She had an awful desire to shock Almaz, to tell her about the arms and legs she'd seen flying through the air in the bombing raids, and what it felt like to be swept down a flooded river in the dark, and how tired you felt after months of eating only the most basic kind of food, and how the camp latrines stank so much you wanted to be sick, and how the man in the cabin next to theirs had screamed and screamed in the night.

"What grade are you in at school?" she asked with an effort.

"Same as you, I suppose."

"Except that I don't go to school any more."

Almaz looked shocked.

"Oh, but you mustn't stop school. I mean your education's so important. Daya wants me to do business studies. She did want me to be a doctor, but I'm hopeless at science, I really am. I might go into insurance or something. You get really well paid if you've got good qualifications."

"But I thought women couldn't do that kind of job here?"

"Yes they can. Mind you, there's a lot of things women can't do. It's not like Sulaimaniya."

Tara detected a hint of disapproval in Almaz's voice, as if she thought Sulaimaniya was too free and easy.

"It's much better in Sulaimaniya!" she said, suddenly flaring up.

"Oh, yes, I didn't mean . . ."

"Kurdish women are free, and they can do proper jobs and everything. You don't get put in prison in Sulaimaniya just for talking to a man like you do here. And look at Kurdish clothes! We don't have to cover ourselves up in these horrible long dresses, and chadors and everything."

"No, of course not." said Almaz, taken aback by Tara's outburst.

There was an awkward silence.

Almaz picked up a comb and ran it through her hair.

"Isn't your brother a student?" she said, trying to find a neutral subject.

"He was."

"What's he doing now?"

"He was called up."

"Is he in the army then?"

"No. He didn't join up. He's in Kurdistan, with the pesh murgas."

"Oh, how awful. Poor him." Almaz was gushing extra hard in her efforts to sound understanding.

"What about yours?" said Tara, trying to respond. "You've got two older brothers, haven't you?"

"Yes," said Almaz. "They were really lucky. They were both studying abroad when the war started. Rezgar's in France and Jwamer's in Norway. I expect they'll stay there till everything's calmed down."

Tara clenched her teeth.

You've got no idea, she thought. No idea at all.

"Would you like to go shopping now?" said Almaz brightly. "There are some lovely new winter clothes in. I've seen some fabulous sweaters in the bazaar at Reza Tabrizi's. Everyone goes there."

Tara stood up with relief.

"Yes, let's go out," she said.

Back in the sitting room, Teriska Khan and Auntie Noor were still sitting side by side, deep in conversation, while Hero, who'd eaten nearly as much as a grown-up, lay fast asleep on a pile of cushions.

"Can I take Tara to the shops, Daya?" said Almaz, lifting her chador down from the peg where it hung behind the door.

"Yes, of course, dear," said Auntie Noor absently, and turned back to Teriska Khan.

"Mind you're back by five o'clock," Teriska Khan called after them. She smiled at Tara. "What a treat for you. Have a lovely time, darling. Have you got the money I gave you?"

"Yes thanks, Daya," said Tara. She knew she ought to be more excited, but somehow, she didn't know why, she couldn't feel anything much.

I've changed, she thought. I'm just not the same kind of person any more.

It was as if something in her had died over the last few months. The young, careless part of herself had withered away. Something else would grow in its place, but it wouldn't be the same. She wasn't a child any longer.

22

The shopping expedition was much more fun than Tara had thought it would be. She started off being almost confused by the huge quantities of things to choose from. Auntie Noor might say that since the war had started you couldn't find a thing in Teheran, but when you hadn't been able to even go into a shop for months the mass of stuff to choose from seemed confusing. Tara had forgotten the feeling of browsing through racks of clothes, and picking out shoes and sweaters from tempting piles, and she didn't know where to start.

Almaz was easier to get on with once they were out of doors. She was obviously enjoying herself, pointing out things that Tara had missed, and hunting around for the right sizes. Tara started liking her a bit better.

By the time they got back to the flat a couple of hours later, Tara had bought a pretty satiny blouse, a warm fluffy sweater with a pattern of flowers all over it, and a skirt that fitted her properly. Best of all she had some decent shoes at long last.

When they opened the front door, everything seemed very quiet. Too quiet in fact.

"Where is everyone?" said Tara.

"Gone out shopping too, I expect," said Almaz unconcernedly. Tara started feeling uneasy. She didn't like not knowing where Daya was.

"Sh!" said Almaz. "What's that?"

They both listened. There was a strange kind of animal noise coming from the sitting room.

"Must be thieves!" whispered Almaz, clutching at Tara's arm. Tara shook her off and opened the sitting room door.

The lunch things had all been cleared up and tidied away, but Teriska Khan and Auntie Noor were back on the cushions where they'd been before, both fast asleep. Their mouths were wide open. Teriska Khan was snoring gently, her breath coming and going easily, but Auntie Noor was rumbling like a volcano every time she breathed in, and when she breathed out again it was with a mighty whistle.

"What is it? Who's there?" hissed Almaz over Tara's shoulder.

Tara was shaking so hard she couldn't answer. She stepped back, and Almaz plucked up her courage to peep in through the door. Then she caught Tara's eye and clapped her hand over her mouth to keep in a shriek of laughter. They fled down the corridor to Almaz's room, flopped down onto her bed and buried their heads in the cushions.

"Did you see my daya's dress all ruckled up? I

could see her bra!"

"Yes, half her buttons have popped open," wailed Tara. "Did you see my mother's gold fillings?"

"No, but I saw her tonsils!"

This seemed so hysterically funny that neither of them could say anything for a good long time. At last Tara sat up and mopped her eyes. She felt better than she had done for months and months.

"I'm going to put on my new clothes," she said.

Five minutes later, she was looking at herself in the mirror. She could hardly believe her eyes. She hadn't really seen herself for six months. In that time she'd slimmed down. Her cheek bones showed now, and her eyebrows seemed more arched and finer. She'd grown a couple of inches, and her figure had changed too. She had a proper bust, and her waist looked thinner. And her hair looked different too. At home she'd always kept it under some sort of control, with slides, or combs or something, and although it had been shoulder length her friend Khadijah at school, who was brilliant at hairdressing, had trimmed it for her regularly. She hadn't been bothering to tie it back lately because it was covered with the regulation scarf whenever she went out, and anyway there hadn't been a mirror anywhere to do it in. Now it waved and curled long and free, round her face and down her back. She wasn't sure whether it looked silly or not.

"Your hair's nice," said Almaz. "I envy you. It's so thick. I have such trouble with mine." She looked in the mirror and patted it complacently. "It's terribly soft and fine. Baby hair, Daya calls it."

Tara turned her head from side to side. Almaz was right. Her hair was nice. She tried pulling it back away from her face. It looked good. She mentally counted up the change she'd had from the money Daya had given her. There'd be enough for some clips and slides anyway. They cost practically nothing.

"Does that sweater fit all right?" asked Almaz.

"Oh, it's lovely," said Tara. She stretched out first one arm then the other to pull the sleeve of the blouse down so that the cuff showed.

"Isn't that wool rather hard?" said Almaz, picking up a bottle of varnish and beginning to touch up her nails. "I can't stand wool next to the skin. I'm funny like that. My skin's really sensitive."

Tara didn't bother to answer. She didn't have to.

"You're pretty," said a voice from the door. Both girls turned round. Hero was standing there. She'd obviously just woken up. She still looked flushed and rumpled, and there were marks on her cheeks from the folds of the cushion she'd been lying on. She was looking at Tara, but Almaz didn't notice that. She smiled, pleased with the compliment, swung her legs off the bed and advanced on Hero enthusiastically.

"Oh, what a little darling you are!" she said. "Sweet little thing! Come on, let's dress you up too."

She tried to take Hero's hand, but Hero wriggled away from her, ran to Tara and hid behind her, holding on tight to her new skirt.

Almaz laughed.

"I've got just the thing for you," she said. "Look!" She opened a drawer and took out a bright green nylon blouse with pearl buttons down the front. It looked several sizes too big for Hero.

"Come on, lovey," she cooed, reaching out a hand towards Hero. "Try it on. You'll look so sweet. Just like a little princess."

Hero looked at her for a long moment and took a firmer grasp of Tara's skirt.

"I can't stand green next to the skin," she said solemnly. "I'm sen-sensitive."

Tara had to turn her face away.

"Oh, don't be silly," said Almaz. "Come here! Almaz will brush your hair for you and put in a pretty ribbon."

Hero edged herself further round behind Tara. Almaz dug into a drawer and pulled out a length of slightly crumpled blue ribbon. She dangled it in front of Hero.

Tara felt a tug on her arm, then Hero slid her fingers down till she found Tara's hand, and held on to it tightly.

"Tara's prettier than you," she said firmly. "Tara's really really really pretty."

Almaz put the ribbon down.

"You're a bit pretty," said Hero kindly.

Almaz laughed, but the laugh had a tinkly sound in it.

"Thank you very much," she said.

"Hero," began Tara, trying hard not to laugh. She felt for the sake of politeness she ought to stem the flow. "Why don't you go and . . ."

But Hero hadn't finished.

"I don't want your ribbon," she said. "I got baby hair. It's terribly soft and fine."

"*Hero!*" said Tara desperately. "Run and see if Daya's awake. I'm sure it's late."

"Daya is awake," said Hero. "She wants you. We've got to go now."

"Why didn't you tell me before?" said Tara, unzipping her new skirt.

"You didn't ask me," said Hero, aggrieved. "Why are you taking your clothes off?"

"Because . . . Oh, I don't have to, do I? Of course, they're mine. I can wear them back to the camp." Tara pushed the pile of old clothes lying on the floor with the toe of her new shoes. "I suppose I'd better take these back with me, though I never want to see them again."

Back in the sitting room, Teriska Khan didn't seem in any real hurry to go. She and Auntie Noor seemed to have taken up their conversation where they'd left off before they fell asleep. Teriska Khan was looking anxious.

"I'm sure Soran will find a way to . . ." she was saying.

"No, really," Auntie Noor stood up, and shook out her skirt. "I don't want to worry you, but they don't usually let people stay near Teheran for long. They send everyone on to that camp down in the desert I was telling you about. The conditions are frightful. It's much worse than the one you were in up in the mountains. Hero would never survive it. And with your health the way it is now . . . Perhaps you should try to go abroad, out of Iran, at least until the war's over. After all, it can't last for ever."

Teriska Khan stood up too.

"We'll see what . . ." she began. Then she saw Tara. "Oh, you look lovely!" she said. "What a nice sweater! And the skirt! How much did all that cost?"

The drive back to the camp seemed very short. It was amazing, thought Tara, how quickly you got used to things again. There was the fruit stall, exactly the same as it had been this morning, but it looked quite ordinary now. The fruit looked smaller, less magical. Teriska Khan had a bagful of it on her lap, which she'd stopped to buy at the little shop at the bottom of Uncle Daban's building. The shops and the buildings looked different too. They were nothing extraordinary. Just shops and buildings, after all. Even the traffic didn't seem so scary now.

Baba and Uncle Daban were having their usual conversation about Kurdish politics in the front of the car. Tara couldn't be bothered to follow it all. Anyway, Hero was demanding all her attention.

"Auntie Noor's house is nice," she was saying,

"especially the toilet. But I like our house better."

"So do I," sighed Tara. "Ours is much bigger."

"No, it isn't," said Hero. "We've only got one room. Auntie Noor's got lots and lots."

"What on earth do you mean?" said Tara. Then she understood. Hero was talking about their hovel in the refugee camp.

"That's not our house," she said. "Our house is at home. You know, in Sulaimaniya."

"Where's that?" said Hero vaguely, watching a man on a bicycle loaded high with boxes and bundles, trying to weave his way through the traffic.

Tara was shocked.

"Don't you remember home?" she said. "Our lovely house, and the beautiful kitchen, and the garden and everything? You used to play in the garden all the time."

"Yes," said Hero, not really listening. "That's what I like. At our house you can go outside, and I can play with Nazim and Raz. We're going to play with the mud again tomorrow. We're going to make little houses."

Tara picked her up and put her on her knee. She couldn't bear to think that Hero had forgotten home already. She hadn't thought about it much before, but she could see now that Hero was having just as hard a time as everyone else. She'd always seemed so bouncy, so pushy in asking for everything she wanted, so full of confidence, and able to twist everyone round her little finger that it was easy to forget how much she was missing too. She'd been three when they'd left home, and now she was already four.

I was at kindergarten when I was her age, thought Tara. And I had my own nice bed, and lots of toys, and a proper house to live in, and I used to go to parties.

She gave Hero a little squeeze.

"Next time we get a permit I'll take you shopping with me," she said, "and we'll get you something really nice."

Hero sat up and looked at her excitedly.

"I want a dress," she said. "I don't want a green blouse. I want a pink dress and it's got to have little sleeves and lots and lots of little flowers all over it."

"Right," said Tara. "There's got to be a dress like that somewhere in Teheran."

"And I don't want brown shoes like the ones Baba got me yesterday," said Hero. "I want shiny black ones, and I want big bows on them and sparkly bits on the toes."

She was still describing the socks, ribbons, jumpers and nightdresses she wanted when the car stopped outside the refugee camp, and they all had to get out and report to the sentry at the gate.

23

Winter, 1984

A few weeks later the snow, which had come months earlier in the mountains, arrived in Teheran. The first fall surprised everyone. Tara opened the creaking rough door of their little room and looked out onto a cold white world.

"There, you see," said Teriska Khan. "Noor was quite right to make us get proper winter shoes and sweaters. You'd better put on those gloves Almaz gave you when you go and get the water. I can't imagine why you made such a fuss about accepting them. It was very kind of her to think of it. And sensible too."

Tara didn't say anything. Daya was right of course. Almaz and Auntie Noor had been kind. Too kind. Every time any of the family came back from a visit to the flat, their bags were stuffed with handed-on clothes, jars of cosmetics and all kinds of little luxuries.

She pulled on the long regulation dress over her bulky woollen sweater and tied the scarf over her head. Then she draped the new chador with the embroidered edging (a cast-off of Auntie Noor's) over it all, opened the door, picked up the clanking enamel bucket by its freezing handle and started plodding through the snow to the standpipe.

At least we won't be here for long, she thought, but it wasn't much of a comfort. The alternatives seemed so scary. She couldn't bear to think about that camp in the south that Auntie Noor was always talking about. Daya wouldn't have a chance in a place like that if she got ill again.

She filled up her bucket and started back, her fingers numb with cold. She should have worn Almaz's gloves after all. What was the sense of being so proud when you hadn't got anything left to be proud about?

At least breakfast was something to look forward to now that they could go out and buy things in the shops. Tara still hadn't started to take for granted the luxury of honey with her bread and sugar in her tea. She was on her third glass when Kak Soran stood up, and began to put on his outdoor clothes.

"I must get going," he said. "I've got to be in Teheran when the offices are opening. There's still a lot of paperwork to see to and you have to wait for hours everywhere."

When Kak Soran came home that night he was pale and drawn. Teriska Khan took one look at him and silently filled a plate with hot tasty stew from the pan that was perched precariously on the tiny paraffin stove. It was obvious that he had bad news. She was in no hurry to hear it.

He ate without much appetite and handed back

his plate half finished. Teriska Khan started to clear away the food, but he put out a hand and stopped her.

"Leave that till later," he said. "Sit down and listen." A year ago he would have nodded to Tara to leave the room, but now it was different. It wasn't only that there was no other room to go to. He wanted her to listen too. She got up from the corner where she'd been taking up the hem of Hero's new dress and sat down beside Teriska Khan. The light of the oil lamp cast a strong glow on her parents' faces.

They look older, she thought with surprise. Kak Soran pressed his hand against his forehead as if he had a headache.

"You're not going to like this, Teriska," he said warningly, "but I might as well tell you straight. We've got to leave Iran now, at once."

"But . . ."

"No, listen. I was talking to Ali and some of the pesh murga leaders today. You remember Hussein, Zhen's brother?"

Teriska Khan nodded impatiently.

"He came over here before we did. The Iranian secret police picked him up last week. They've forced out of him details about the factory he worked in, its location, output – all that kind of thing. They bombed it yesterday. The whole place went up in smoke. Dozens of workers were killed. Ali says it's only a matter of time before they get on to me. My factory was a lot more important. Just the sort of vital installation the Iranians would like to destroy."

A moth had got into the little room. It was beating its wings helplessly against the glass shade of the oil lamp. Tara could hardly bear to watch it.

"Well, but Soran," Teriska Khan was saying, "even if they did ask you . . ."

"Ask!" he laughed shortly. "They wouldn't be so polite, believe me. Just think about it. Think what it would mean. If they bomb my factory it's not the government of Iraq that would suffer, it's the people. Our own friends and neighbours. We may have taken refuge in Iran but we're still Iraqis. I'm not going to help Iran bomb our country – betray all the people I've known and worked with all these years."

Mr Mahmoud, thought Tara. He'd be killed. He risked his life for us.

"We must leave now, at once," Kak Soran said.

Teriska Khan was speechless. She couldn't take it in.

"Leave Iran at once?" she said stupidly. "What do you mean? Where can we go?"

"I'm seeing Daban first thing in the morning. He said his son was going to phone tonight from Paris. He thinks he might be able to help us get temporary visas for France."

France! Tara shivered. She was feeling numb. The familiar knot of fear was tying itself inside her stomach again. It had been awful in Iran, but at least she'd felt that Baba was safe. But now they were on the run again. There was to be no stopping here after all. They'd have to pick themselves up and go on again, to somewhere even stranger and further away.

But France! It sounded so cold and foreign and distant. She tried to imagine France, but she couldn't. Now she'd lived in Teheran she could see the rest of Iran quite easily in her mind's eye. She could guess what kinds of shops and houses and mosques there'd be, and what the people would be like. And she could imagine other countries nearer home like Turkey and Syria and the Gulf States a bit too. She knew lots of people, Kurds and others, who'd lived there. But she couldn't imagine what France was like at all.

Next day Kak Soran came home earlier than usual. He sat down heavily on a cushion and stretched out his hands to warm them at the tiny paraffin stove.

"Daban's boy Rezgar did phone last night," he said wearily. "France is out of the question. They've tightened up on refugees. I've heard the same story all over the place. It's going to be incredibly difficult to get in anywhere. Germany, Sweden, Norway, Britain – they take a few, then they bring the shutters down again."

"What about Canada?" said Tara anxiously. She'd spent hours listening to Daya who'd been talking all day to the other women in the camp, discussing every possible country in the world that could be a new destination. Of them all, she'd liked the sound of Canada best.

"Canada?" Kak Soran shrugged. "Forget it. It's

almost as hopeless as the United States, and you might as well try to get to the moon as get in there. We'll just have to get our exit papers in order, and get on a flight to Europe, and claim asylum wherever we can."

"But we can't do that!" burst out Teriska Khan. "What about Ashti? He'd never be able to trace us."

"Don't worry about Ashti. I've arranged all that with Daban. We've sent a message through to him telling him we're going out. Once it's safe for him to come through to Iran Daban will look after him. He'll get him any money he needs, and be our contact with him. It's the best I can arrange."

Teriska Khan was looking more and more agitated.

"But we can't go to any European country just like that! They might refuse to take us, or send us on somewhere else. The stories I've heard! People sometimes go travelling round for weeks, from one airport to another, not allowed to stop anywhere!"

"What on earth do you want then?" Kak Soran was obviously losing his patience. Tara could see his teeth were clenched. "Do you want to go to the desert camp in the south? Do you want the Iranian police to torture information out of me and bomb my old factory and everyone in it? Or perhaps you'd like them to send us back to Iraq, where I'd be executed straight away, and you'd be sent to prison! Wake up, Teriska. This is the only thing we can do. We just haven't got any choice."

It was funny, thought Tara, when she woke up the next morning, how quickly a new idea became an old one. Last night the thought of going to Europe had been so strange and scary she hadn't been able to take it in at all, but this morning her brain seemed to accept it, and she had to start bracing herself to face a whole new life, an extraordinary, unfamiliar future.

The next few days dragged by. Every moment was filled with tension. When Baba went off to Teheran each morning, Tara never knew if he'd come back that night. And every evening, when he did come home, he'd be fretting and fuming at the time it was taking to get their papers sorted out, and the huge sums of money he was expected to pay to get them all safely away.

By the time they were actually ready to go, with their papers in some kind of order, their exit permits for the camp arranged, and airtickets to London booked and paid for, he was looking thin and haggard. Every last penny of the money they had so carefully smuggled over the mountains and through the camps had gone. Nothing remained except some pieces of jewellery.

Uncle Daban drove them to the airport. They'd been discharged from the camp the day before, and had spent the night in their cousins' flat. There had hardly been time to go to bed. They had to be at the airport by six o'clock in the morning. They sat in silence in the car, except for

Hero who was excited at the thought of going on a plane.

"Will it bump when it hits the clouds?" she said nervously.

"Of course not," said Tara, but she didn't feel as sure as she sounded. She couldn't imagine flying through clouds.

Kak Soran and Teriska Khan were under such strain that Tara could almost feel the tension radiating out from them. Her own stomach was churning too.

"This is our one and only chance," she'd heard her father say to Uncle Daban. "Our tickets are only valid for this flight. If they arrest me at the airport, or if we miss our plane somehow, we'll lose them and all the money, and I'll never get enough together to try again."

Tara tried not to think about it. She tried to look at the beautiful buildings and gardens of Teheran as they flashed past in the half-light of dawn. It was sad to say goodbye.

We could have made a good life here, she thought. We could have settled down and made friends and been happy.

The airport was very crowded. It was obvious here that a war was going on. Soldiers were everywhere and security was very tight. Uncle Daban nudged Kak Soran.

"It's not the ones in uniform you have to watch out for," he whispered. "It's the revolutionary guards."

Tara clutched her chador even more tightly

under her chin and looked round nervously. She didn't need anyone to tell her which the revolutionary guards were. You could pick them out at once. They were all young and looked stern and humourless. Most of them had beards and they had their shirts buttoned up to the neck under their dark jackets but didn't wear any ties. Some carried radios, and kept talking into them. Some were armed. But the most obvious thing about them was their arrogant self-assurance. They could do what they liked here. They could stop and search anyone. They could confiscate papers and money. They could hold you up and make you miss your plane if they decided they didn't like the look of you. They had power, and they looked as if they were enjoying it.

"Do whatever they tell you," Kak Soran said quietly to Tara and Teriska Khan. "Don't draw attention to yourself, and try to keep Hero quiet. Thank God we have plenty of time before the flight leaves, so if there is a hitch . . ."

There wasn't. To everyone's huge relief they were checked out through the official desks, their luggage was only lightly searched and after a tearful farewell to Uncle Daban and hours of tension and boredom in the departure lounge, where everyone looked like a secret policeman in disguise, they found themselves on the plane at last, strapped into their seats, and were taxiing onto the runway.

The plane was due to make a stopover at Munich.

"It's a good place to go to," Uncle Daban had said. "If they don't let you into Britain they'll probably send you back to the last place you came from, and you've got a better chance of getting asylum in Germany than in most other places."

Kak Soran had agreed with that. He had several Kurdish friends in Germany already, and his pocket book was stuffed with their addresses.

The plane roared up into the air. Tara had never flown before. She liked the comfortable seats and the meal in its neat little tray, but she couldn't sit back and enjoy it. The uncertainty was too awful. This journey was like going into a long dark tunnel, not knowing where the other end would come out. Where would she sleep tonight? In which country? In what kind of bed? Or would it be on the floor in some impersonal airport lounge? And once in London, would they be allowed to stay there, or would they be put straight back onto a plane, to Munich perhaps, or back to Teheran, or even worse, to Baghdad?

For a while she managed to doze, then at last the flight attendant spoke over the aircraft intercom. He gave the message twice, once in German and once in Persian. Tara picked out a word or two of the Persian, but she couldn't really understand it.

"What's he saying?" she said to Kak Soran. He'd often flown in an aeroplane before and he could speak quite good Persian now, after his months in Iran.

"I wasn't listening," he said, "but the plane's going down. Can't you feel it? I think we're about to land."

There was a jerk as the wheels were lowered, and a few minutes later Tara saw the ground outside rushing up to meet them. She craned her neck to see past her parents and look out of the window. She couldn't see much. It was a cloudy day, with a little sunshine straggling through in patches. The airport buildings looked dull and official, and there seemed to be miles of flat tarmac runway. It looked rather grey and impersonal.

Nothing much happened at Munich. The officials looked closely at their papers, and there was a nasty moment when one of them summoned his chief to check through them more carefully, but the tickets were in order, and Kak Soran's Iraqi passport, which dated from long before the war, was still a few months short of its renewal date. They only had to spend a few minutes in the transit lounge before they were called to go on board again.

Quite a few of the original passengers had gone. Their places were mainly taken by middle-aged men with briefcases, who wore smart dark suits and carried winter coats over their arms. They kept looking impatiently at their watches as if every moment was tremendously important. None of them seemed to see the tired family in foreign clothes. They looked right through them.

The flight from Munich to London took no

time at all. The flight attendant barely had time to bring round the trolleys, hand out the snack trays and clear them all away again. Tara ate some of the plastic wrapped food but she saw that Teriska Khan and Kak Soran pushed theirs away unopened.

"Aren't you hungry, Daya?" she said, suddenly worried in case Teriska Khan was going to be ill again.

"No, I couldn't eat a thing," said Teriska Khan with a shudder. Her voice was high-pitched with tension. It gave Tara a jolt and she suddenly found that she wasn't hungry either. The next few hours would be critical for all of them. Their fate, one way or the other, would be decided and they would be powerless to do anything to help themselves. The decision would be made by strangers, English people, who knew nothing about them and couldn't even speak the same language.

Kak Soran had reset his watch to London time, and though it only said 5 o'clock it was quite dark outside.

"Are you sure it's so early?" said Teriska Khan, peering out of the window to the long lines of lights that marked the runway at Heathrow airport. "It's completely dark already."

Kak Soran didn't answer. He was too busy folding his little table away. The plane was about to land.

It was a long time before the plane stopped moving, but as soon as it did people started getting up from their seats and pulling their coats and bags out of the overhead lockers. There was the usual cheerful buzz of chatter. Everyone was glad to be back on firm ground. Tara started to get up too.

"Don't hurry," said Kak Soran quietly. "Stay where you are for a bit. We're going to take as long as we can. If they look at our papers straightaway they could send us off again at once in this plane. This flight goes on to New York in half an hour. If we hang about till it takes off they'll have to let us through, at least for tonight."

It wasn't difficult to go slowly. Hero had fallen asleep, and had to be carried. It seemed quite normal to wait until everyone else was off the plane so that she wouldn't be jogged awake.

When they eventually got out into the airport corridor, they were at the tail end of the crowd of passengers, who were hurrying towards the immigration controls, keen to get through and out into the baggage hall to collect their things. Tara looked at them curiously. She'd forgotten how bright and different women looked without the scarves and dull, long, button-through dresses and chadors that covered them from head to foot in Iran.

"Go slower," said Kak Soran, looking round. They were moving too fast. They needed to take much more time if they were to give the plane a chance to take off before they got to the immigration desk. But they looked conspicuous, dawdling along an empty corridor, miles behind the other passengers.

Just then some doors behind them opened and a clatter of feet came down the corridor. Another plane had landed and the passengers were pouring off it. Kak Soran and his family kept moving very slowly, feeling protected by the crowd milling past them, stopping all the time to put down their hand luggage as though it weighed too much. The stream of passengers seemed never-ending.

"Must have been a big plane," muttered Teriska Khan. "Do you think it's safe yet? Can we go on?"

Kak Soran shook his head.

"The longer we leave it the better," he said. "Just go on looking as if you're walking, but move as slowly as you can."

It was a busy day at Heathrow. Planeload after planeload of passengers seemed to be landing. Tara could see that they came from different countries. Some people were obviously from the Far East. There were women wearing saris and men with turbans. There was a group of Chinese or Japanese people, and another planeload from somewhere in America.

It was a good thing, thought Tara, that they had so many passengers to hide among. The lights overhead were dazzlingly bright, the floors hard and shiny, the walls bare and straight. Not even a fly would have found a place to hide here.

A man in uniform came slowly down the

corridor. He looked hard at Kak Soran and said something in English. Kak Soran spread out his hands to show he didn't understand.

"I suppose we'd better go on now," he said to Teriska Khan. "I think that man came past here a while ago. He's probably watching us. I should think there's quite a queue waiting to go through by this time. There must be a plane landing every few minutes. Anyway, ours must be taking off again very soon now."

In the immigration hall the queues looked encouragingly long. Kak Soran made for the longest. It moved slowly towards a high desk at the end of which a woman in uniform was sitting.

Tara's heart was thudding. What on earth would happen to them now? Would they be allowed through? Would they be sent off on another plane? And if they did get through where would they go? How on earth would they get started in this strange country when they couldn't even speak the language?

She looked round the big hall. There were some large bright advertisement posters lit from behind. The slogans in huge English letters screamed to be read. She could pick out a few words, but she couldn't understand the meanings.

"I wish I'd tried harder in English lessons at school," she thought.

She heard a burst of laughter and turned her head. It came from the next queue, where there was a group of young people. They were making a lot of noise, shouting and laughing. They all seemed to know each other, as if they'd been travelling together. Tara stared at them. They'd obviously been to a hot country, because some of them were still wearing summer clothes although it looked cold and wintry outside. One boy was even wearing shorts. And the girl behind him had next to nothing on – a really short skirt and a blouse that showed her shoulders and plunged right down back and front.

Tara felt a slow, hot blush spread over her face. She'd never in her life seen people dressed so indecently, or behaving so noisily in public. And what were they doing now? Right here, where anyone could see them, the boy had draped his bare arm round the girl's bare neck, and he was bending his head over as if he was going to kiss her! Tara felt too ashamed and embarrassed for them to go on looking.

In any case, they were nearly at the head of the queue now. Tara looked at her parents. Kak Soran was holding his papers tightly. Tara saw him bite his lower lip. He was blinking nervously, trying to see what kind of a person the impassive woman in the dark uniform might be. Teriska Khan's face looked calm and dignified, like on the night Rostam had come, and she'd thought the police were at the door. You could only tell how nervous she was because the jingling of her bangles showed how much her arms were trembling as she held the dead weight of Hero on her shoulder.

The people in front of them went through the

narrow gap past the immigration officer. Teriska Khan gave Kak Soran a little shove with her elbow.

"Go on," she hissed.

Kak Soran put his papers down in front of the official. The woman's eyes flickered up from them to Kak Soran's face. He'd rehearsed what he was meant to say.

"Refugee," he said. "Asylum."

The woman didn't say anything. She flicked through the papers in front of her. They were in Arabic lettering and she couldn't read them. But she studied the photograph and looked over to Teriska Khan and Tara. She asked a question. Kak Soran guessed she was asking if they were a family, and nodded.

The woman eased herself out of her chair and stood up. The people in the queue behind shifted and muttered. They could see there was going to be a hold up. The official beckoned to Kak Soran to follow her, and went across to a door. She opened it, and shouted to someone inside.

"Mike! Got a nice Christmas present for you. Asylum seekers. Family of four. The man's pretending he can't speak a word of English but he looks a bit dodgy to me."

Then she jerked her head at Kak Soran, who guessed at her meaning and went through the door, and the others followed him into a brightly lit, bare room.

24

During the last few days in Teheran, and especially while she'd been on the plane, Tara had tried to imagine what England would be like. It was easier to picture than Germany because she'd once seen a film on TV which showed a lot of big famous buildings in London, like Buckingham Palace, and Westminster. Everyone in the film had looked rich and comfortable, and they'd done all kinds of things you couldn't possibly do in Iraq or Iran, like drink alcohol right out in the open where anyone could see them, and dance, men and women together, in public places, and walk out into the street at night. Tara had often been out after dark at home, but only in the car. Since the pesh murgas had started their activities no one would have been mad enough to walk round the streets of Sulaimaniya after night had fallen.

London had looked like a beautiful city, full of happy, busy people. Of course, she knew it was cold and rained all the time, but then everyone lived in such big nice houses it probably didn't matter much.

English people, she thought vaguely, would be all blond with blue eyes and they'd be rather cool and polite, and have plenty of money and good jobs. And they'd dress rather like the Queen or Princess Diana, whose picture she'd often seen at home.

What she hadn't expected was that arriving in London would be rather like arriving in that first tiny village in Iran the night they'd ridden through the mountains.

First there was the same long, long wait while nobody came. They were all tired and edgy, and the little room, which didn't have a window, got very hot and stuffy. Every now and then the door would open and a big man with thin greasy hair would look in, and say something. Once a girl came with a tray of cups full of an orangey brown liquid.

"Tea," she said, smiling brightly at them.

Tara thought she recognised the English word.

"I think it's supposed to be tea," she said, picking up a cup by its handle and gingerly trying it. She was used to drinking tea out of little tea glasses, and the thick white china felt strange.

"It doesn't taste much like tea," she said doubtfully. "It's very bitter."

Kak Soran opened a paper sachet that was on the tray and tested the contents with his finger. "Sugar," he said. "Put some in. We'd better try to drink it whatever it tastes like. We mightn't get anything else for hours."

Eventually the door opened again and two

people came into the room. One was the big man with greasy hair. He didn't look at them. He sat down behind a desk and put a stack of forms down on the table. Tara noticed that his finger nails were dirty.

There was a woman with him. She was wearing a navy blue suit with a short skirt that hardly covered her knees. She sat down beside the man, and Tara realized that she was an official person too, one of the immigration officers.

Tara could hardly drag her eyes away from her. It wasn't just the bold way she was dressed that was so surprising, it was the way she moved, so confidently and easily, as if she was in her own home. And she talked to the man just like another man would have done. She could have been his equal, or even his boss! Now she was staring at Baba, quite openly, in a way a woman would never have dared look at a man at home, and as she did so she crossed and uncrossed her legs as if she wasn't even aware that her knees were showing.

After a while the woman said something to the man that sounded like an order, and he got up and went out. He came back after a moment with two of the family's suitcases.

"Oh, thank goodness, here's our stuff," said Teriska Khan. "I was worried sick they'd lost it, or confiscated it or something. Where's the rest?"

From where he was sitting Kak Soran could see out through the open door.

"It's all here, I think," he said, looking

relieved too.

Another man, darker than the others, came into the room.

"Are you Kurdish? Which dialect do you speak?" he said to Kak Soran.

Tara jumped. The man had actually spoken in Kurdish!

Kak Soran looked relieved. He smiled broadly and held out his hand.

"Oh, yes, we're Kurds," he said. "We speak Sorani."

The man shook his hand briefly, and looked away.

"I'm the interpreter," he said, sitting down next to the woman, as far away from Kak Soran as he could.

"What's happening? What are they going to do about us?" said Kak Soran hurriedly. Tara hated hearing the anxiety in his voice. It made her feel more nervous than anything else could have done.

"I don't know," said the interpreter coolly. "You'll have to wait and see." He looked towards the woman and nodded to her. Kak Soran understood. This person might look Middle Eastern, and speak Kurdish (though he had a funny accent as though Kurdish wasn't his first language) but he was an official, like the others. There was no point in trying to make friends with him.

The questions seemed to go on for ages and ages. Tara almost wished they were back in Iran. This woman interviewer was the hardest and coldest they'd ever had. Her questions seemed to pound at Kak Soran, as if she was trying all the time to trip him up, to make him say something incriminating. Tara could hardly bear to listen. Baba sounded so humble, and frightened, so unlike his real self.

She leaned back and looked at the wall above the woman's desk. There were some cards stuck onto it with bright coloured pictures on them. There was one of a triangular shaped tree with decorations and lights all over it. Another showed a little bird with a brown back and a red breast perched on a snowy twig, and there were several of a big man with a white beard all dressed in red, with a sack over his shoulders.

The searches, when they started, were much worse than they'd been in Iran. The two men doing it seemed to know by instinct where things would be hidden, and they went straight for them. Tara couldn't help gasping in dismay when first Daya's heavy gold necklace was pulled out of a cunning cavity in the heel of a shoe, and then her diamond earrings were dug out of the jar of face cream she'd embedded them in.

Teriska Khan turned a white face to Kak Soran. "We're ruined," she whispered.

Tara felt her heart drop into her boots, but then it lifted again. The searchers didn't seem interested in the jewellery. They were actually putting it back into the suitcase! The only thing they seemed to want was a tin of white antibiotic powder that Auntie Noor had given Teriska Khan to dust over Hero's foot, where there was a sore red place that was taking a long time to heal. One of them looked at it closely, and showed it to the other, who nodded, wrapped it carefully in a plastic bag and took it out of the room.

At last it was all over, and they were left alone again. Teriska Khan's nerves were reaching snapping point.

"Are we going to be here for ever?" she wailed. "Oh God, what's going to happen now? At least in Iran there are other Kurds, and we had relatives there. But here we're all alone! If we don't get out of this room soon, I'm going to scream!"

Her tension was catching. Tara began to feel a knot tightening in her own stomach, and her hands were clammy with a nervous sweat. Hero, who'd been amazingly quiet and subdued all this time, suddenly jumped up and banged her arm on the side of the metal desk. The pain made her scream, and once she'd started she couldn't stop, and went on and on crying.

It seemed like several more hours before the interpreter came back, though it was only forty minutes by the electric clock over the door.

"Please, can't you tell us anything?" Teriska Khan pleaded with him.

The interpreter's face cracked into the shadow of a smile.

"You're lucky," he said. "They wanted to send you back to Munich on this evening's plane, but it's taken off now, so you'll be staying tonight at least. It'll give you a chance to see the people who can help you. There'll be transport along in a minute to take you to the detention centre at Harmondsworth until they decide what to do with you. Don't worry. You're over the first hurdle."

He hurried off as if he was afraid of being caught talking to them on his own.

It seemed to Tara as she picked up her share of the bags and bundles and trudged down the endlessly long corridor after her parents and Hero that she'd been travelling for ever and ever.

There was a big glass window on one side of the corridor. Through it she could see some kind of a VIP lounge. There was a proper carpet, and she could see big potted plants, and tall well-dressed businessmen sipping drinks and reading magazines while they lounged on plushy sofas and chairs. It had the kind of comfort and the kind of furniture she'd always been used to before they left home. Once again, she was on the outside looking in.

The strap of her bundle dug into her shoulder. She shifted it to the other side, and went on. At the end of the corridor a flight of steps led down to a door.

It was cold outside, not the crisp, dry coldness of Teheran in winter, but an awful dank, seeping coldness that seemed to go right through you. And there, pulled up at the pavement, was a minibus, just like the one that had taken them from the border to the mountains, and from the mountains to Teheran.

There wasn't much point in trying to see anything of England out of the window. For one thing it was dark, for another it was raining, and anyway there wasn't much to see except for roads, and car headlights, and a lot of modern airport buildings. And when they got to the detention centre it had that same prison feel as a refugee camp, with a barbed wire fence all round it, and uniformed guards at the door.

The first thing Tara noticed when she got inside was the heat. She gave one last big shiver to throw off the cold, and felt the warmth go right through her. But the next thing she noticed was the smell. It was an old, tired, hospital kind of smell. The building seemed clean enough, although it was very plain and shabby, but it was as if years and years of cheap polish and disinfectants had ingrained themselves in the hard vinyl floors and crude brick walls that were covered with thick layers of cream paint. And on top of the hospital smell was a strong whiff of cooking, a kind of strange, foreign cooking that Tara didn't like at all.

A door opened at the end of the corridor, and through it came a group of people, a couple of young African men and a Chinese looking couple. Tara stared at them. She'd never met anyone from the Far East before. She had no idea what they were like, or what kind of customs they had. And although she'd often seen black people in Iraq, she'd never met any Africans. These two men were talking excitedly in a language she didn't recognise, and they walked in a free, dancing kind of way, swinging their arms. She tugged Teriska Khan's sleeve.

"Do you think they're staying here too?" she whispered.

"How should I know?" said Teriska Khan irritably.

They're probably not even Muslims, thought Tara with a sense of panic. We'll have to be really careful what we eat here. That awful smell might be pork cooking.

Everyone slept badly that night. The heat, which had been so welcome when they'd come in out of the cold, was stifling in the bare, comfortless rooms. Tara hardly dared to close her eyes. She hated the idea of being locked into this place with so many strange people. During the evening she hadn't seen anyone else from the Middle East, except for a couple of sad looking Turks who didn't speak Arabic. All the others came from distant countries and nearly all of them were men. They all seemed strung up and distressed, as if they were desperately worried and living on their nerves. She knew what that felt like. She felt the same herself. She was scared a fight would break out, or that someone would break down, and lose control. She was scared she'd be attacked. If that happened she was sure the English guards wouldn't be any use. In a way they were the most frightening people of all. They looked at you as if you weren't there. Their faces

250

were closed and disapproving. Tara hunted round for a way to describe them.

"They *despise* us," she said to herself at last. "That's what it is. They think we're rubbish." It was a horrible thought. The soldiers in Iran had never been friendly, and they hadn't shown the refugees much kindness, but at least they'd look at them as if they were human beings.

The thought of spending days or even weeks in this place was so depressing that the whole family felt miserable the next day. Teriska Khan was worried about Hero, who was hot and flushed and seemed to be running a temperature. Kak Soran took to striding up and down the corridor like a caged animal, glaring at anyone who got in his way.

Then suddenly everything changed. One of the guards, the only one that seemed to have a friendly side to him, put his head round the door of the TV room where half a dozen people were listlessly watching a Walt Disney cartoon.

"Soran!" he said. Kak Soran's head jerked round.

"Telephone," said the man, and mimed holding a receiver to his ear.

Ten minutes later, Kak Soran was back, beaming from ear to ear.

"You'll never believe this," he said. "I can't believe it myself. That was Latif Karwan. You know, my cousin's son. He's studying here, doing a PhD in engineering. I thought he'd gone home months ago, but apparently he's got another year to do."

Teriska Khan had sat up in her chair and was looking at him, astonished.

"But how on earth did he know we were here?"

Kak Soran chuckled.

"That's the extraordinary bit," he said. "Daban's son, Rezgar, phoned Teheran from Paris last night, and Daban told him we'd left to come to London. Latif and Rezgar were children at school together. They know each other well. So Rezgar phoned Latif straight away, and Latif phoned the immigration people first thing this morning, and he finally tracked us down here.

"He says he's got a flat here! It's quite small, but there's only him in it, and he's invited us all to stay with him for as long as we like, until we know whether they'll let us stay in the country or not! Then he'll help us to get a place of our own, and all that kind of thing. And he says he's got a friend in an international bank who'll help me get my money out of Iraq. Isn't that great?"

Teriska Khan burst into tears.

"But how can we go and stay with him, Baba? They won't let us out of here, will they?" said Tara.

Kak Soran interlaced his fingers and bent the joints back so that they all cracked in the way he always did when he was enjoying himself.

"Latif seems to think they will," he said. "He's been through this asylum business with some other friends of his. He's going to speak to the lawyers for us, arrange it all – oh, I can hardly believe it!"

"Does that mean we're going to be allowed to stay in England?" said Tara.

"It's much too soon to say," said Kak Soran looking out of the window at a sodden patch of dusty grass between two shabby old buildings. "There'll be all kinds of questions and interviews and court cases, but we've got a chance, Latif says."

Tara looked out of the window too. She supposed she ought to be glad and excited at the idea that their travels might be over, but all she could think about was that awful smell of foreign cooking that was getting stronger and stronger as the meal time approached.

25

Tara hadn't really believed in Latif. It seemed impossible that here, in this strange country, thousands of miles away from home, a friendly Kurd would be able to come and help them, would actually be allowed in through the high wire fences and the locked doors, past the scornful guards with the big bunches of keys swinging from their belts, and would be able to just sign them out and take them away.

It didn't happen quite like that. There was a long pause while first one of the officials and then Kak Soran spoke on the telephone, and then the interpreter arrived and there was an endless wait while Kak Soran and Teriska Khan sat and answered questions in an airless little office, and Latif had to give all his details and sign a bunch of documents.

But at last, hours later, they were walking down the corridor and out into London itself. The last thing Tara heard as the door of the detention centre swung shut behind them was a frantic row breaking out between two men who both desperately wanted to use the telephone, and the last thing she saw was the face of a little girl, from Vietnam Baba had said, who was standing at the window sadly watching them go.

Tara never forgot that first drive from Harmondsworth to Latif's flat on the other side of London. For one thing, she couldn't believe how big London was. It went on and on for ever, mile after mile of little houses, with their funny patches of front garden and their rows of chimneypots. She couldn't imagine how people could ever find their way in such a maze of streets, when one looked so like another.

Everything she saw was different from what she'd been used to. Everything was a shock. The shops had different kinds of window displays. The house fronts looked more kind of open. You could actually look right into some people's rooms through the uncurtained windows.

There weren't many smart, modern buildings like in Baghdad. Most were rather old and shabby, and some had advertisements on them, huge pictures of cars, or wine bottles, or just lines of writing, or foreign beaches. Lots of them had pictures of women in revealing clothes that were really indecent.

Strangest of all were the people. It was quite cold of course, so nearly everyone was muffled up in thick coats and jackets, but try as she might Tara could see hardly anyone who looked like the sort of English person she'd imagined. Most people looked dowdy, and a lot of them looked quite poor. None of the women were wearing smart coats and hats like the royal family, and a lot of people didn't even look English. In some streets almost everyone was either black or Indian. She couldn't understand it at all.

Latif's flat, when they finally got to it, was the biggest shock. He seemed very pleased with it. He said it was almost impossible to find a place as nice as this in London for the rent he could afford to pay, and he showed them round the small sitting room and two tiny bedrooms with pride.

Tara could hardly hide her disappointment. She'd expected an English flat to be really splendid, much better than Uncle Daban's in Teheran. She had known it would be smaller than the house at home of course, but she'd thought it would still be big enough to sleep them all comfortably and have a nice room to sit and relax in as well.

She looked round disbelievingly at the stained carpet and scarred wooden chairs while Latif talked cheerfully about how he could sleep on the sofa in the sitting room, and the girls could have one bedroom and Teriska Khan and Kak Soran the other. Kak Soran said how much they appreciated it and how kind Latif was, and Teriska Khan butted in to say how she was going to cook him a proper Kurdish dinner just like his own mother would have done.

"That reminds me," she said looking worried. "We'd better go out and do a bit of shopping if we want to eat this evening."

There was an embarrassed silence. Tara saw

Kak Soran frowning at his wife, and they both looked away from Latif. He seemed puzzled for a moment, then he laughed.

"You'll need some English money," he said. "Have you . . ." he paused delicately.

"I've got no money with me at all," said Kak Soran bluntly, spreading out his hands. "I had to spend every penny getting our papers and buying our plane tickets. We've got a lot of stuff still tied up in Sulaimaniya, the house, several bank accounts and so on, but until I can get my hands on that . . ."

"We've got my jewellery," said Teriska Khan firmly, "and I intend to sell it."

She fished down inside her collar and pulled out her necklace.

"Look at that," she said. "Solid gold."

"That's easy," said Latif cheerfully. "Give it to me. I know a friendly jeweller near here. He'll price it for you. And in the meantime — " he pulled out a wad of notes. "I went to the bank this morning. I thought you'd need a bit of ready cash. No, don't worry. You can pay me any time. Ready? Let's go."

Tara stepped out into an English street for the first time in her life with her heart in her mouth. She was quite scared. It was like being in a jungle full of wild animals. You didn't know which way they'd jump.

Latif and Kak Soran led the way, and the others followed. Latif was really confident. He seemed to think it was quite normal that the traffic was going the wrong way, driving on the left instead of on the right. He didn't look twice at the woman who was standing outside a shop shouting at her small child in a loud voice, not caring if anyone was looking or not. He didn't even notice the couple at the bus stop who were gazing at each other in a very frank way and actually holding hands. The girl was wearing a skirt right up above her knees and her hair was brushed up in a kind of spiky fuzz. The boy looked very young, not old enough to be married or anything.

This must be a really bad area, where that kind of woman gets men, thought Tara, trying not to look. But then in front of her she heard Latif say,

"This isn't a bad part of London to live in. Prices are quite reasonable and it's fairly quiet and residential. Plenty of schools for the girls. It's not rough like some places. You could do worse than look for a place of your own round here."

They were almost at the shops now. Tara was relieved. She'd felt uncomfortable in the street. The thick jacket and skirt she'd bought in Teheran didn't look any different from what other people were wearing but she still felt horribly conspicuous as if she was half naked, or luminous or something.

"It feels funny not wearing a chador," she whispered to Teriska Khan.

Teriska Khan squeezed her arm.

"I know," she said. "I feel strange too."

"I suppose you get used to it," said Tara

doubtfully. After all, she'd hated wearing a chador at first. It was only gradually that she'd come to appreciate the feeling it gave you of being safe and private. In Iran everyone respected a woman in a chador. You could go where you liked quite safely. No one would even seem to see you. It was like being invisible. You'd never get cheeky looks or rude comments. But here it was the other way round. No one took any notice of those two girls who were chasing each other down the street, shouting, or at that poor old woman who was mumbling to herself and looking in a litter bin, but she felt sure they'd look at a woman in a veil.

The food shop Latif took them to was a little supermarket. You had to choose things yourself off the shelves and put them in a basket, then pay on the way out. Tara was relieved. They'd never have been able to explain what they wanted to a shopkeeper.

"We'll come back and meet you here," Latif said casually. "I'll take Soran on to see the jeweller. It's only a bit further on from here."

"I want to go with Baba," said Hero, dropping Teriska Khan's hand and catching hold of Kak Soran's. She was the only one, thought Tara enviously, who didn't seem at all surprised by England. Her fever seemed to have miraculously disappeared as soon as they'd left that awful prison place. She skipped off happily with the men, singing a little song to herself.

There were five or six people in the shop. None

of them seemed to know each other and they were all in a tremendous hurry, filling their wire baskets and standing impatiently in a line to pay. No one stopped to chat with the shopkeeper as they would have done at home. No one talked at all, in fact.

Teriska Khan stood helplessly in front of a shelf full of tins and packets.

"I don't know what all this stuff is," she said. "Which is tea and where's the sugar? I can't read the writing and the pictures are so peculiar. Why do all these tins have dogs and cats on them? And how do I know if anything's got pork in it?"

Tara stared at the bright rows of tins and packets. The words in bold Roman letters seemed to stare back at her.

"Winnalot, Whiskas, Pedigree Chum," they said. "Go on, make sense of that."

She passed on to an array of bottles. Some were familiar. You couldn't mistake the Pepsi Cola or the Seven-up. But what about that pale stuff labelled "Lemon Barley Water", and the bottles next to it which read "Orange Squash"? Perhaps they had alcohol in them.

Tara began to feel a bit desperate. It was like being in a maze when you didn't know the way out. She looked along a row of packets. They had pictures of strange desserts on them in brilliant pinks and greens and oranges, and there were closely printed instructions on the back.

Then all of a sudden, Tara felt angry. She moved round the stand to where Teriska Khan was helplessly examining a packet of what might have been sugar, or flour. Tara took it out of her hands, ran her finger down the paper seam and licked it.

"Flour," she said, and put it in Teriska Khan's basket. Then with a new determination she started going systematically along each shelf. She wasn't going to let this place beat her. She was going to learn English, to find her way about, be in control, hold her own. She'd start by getting this shopping sorted out if it killed her.

Teriska Khan had moved over to a stand of vegetables. She was fingering the potatoes and waiting for the shopkeeper to come and serve her. A woman brushed past impatiently. She pulled a polythene bag off a roll and started filling it with oranges. Then she put it in her basket, got another bag and started on the apples. Tara watched her.

"Look, Daya," she said. "You have to do it yourself," and she tore off a polythene bag and began to look over the onions.

The basket was soon quite full.

"We'd better go and get him to weigh it," said Tara, leading the way to the checkout. Teriska Khan put it down on the counter and they both saw the shop keeper for the first time. He was quite dark skinned, like an Indian or a Pakistani.

Without thinking, Teriska Khan spoke in Arabic, like she always did to her usual shopkeeper at home.

"How much is all this then?" she said.

Teriska Khan and Tara looked at each other in amazement. He spoke Arabic too!

"Where do you come from?" asked Teriska Khan eagerly. The man smiled.

"Slowly, please," he said. Obviously his Arabic wasn't very good.

"What country do you come from?" said Teriska Khan.

"Pakistan," said the man. "I speak a little Arabic only."

"You're a Muslim?"

"Yes, of course."

Teriska Khan breathed a sigh of relief.

"Thank God," she said. "Now I can do my shopping. The vegetables are no problem, we've got those. But we need tea, coffee, sugar, spices, milk, butter – all kinds of things. And then there's meat and oil. How do we know if they're OK for Muslims or not?"

By the time Kak Soran and Latif came back, Teriska Khan had two large plastic carrier bags bulging with food.

"I'm going to do the first decent bit of cooking I've been able to do since we left Kurdistan," she said. She looked so determined and defiant that right there, outside the shop on the pavement, they all burst out laughing.

It was as if the sun had come out, thought Tara. She looked round, feeling a bit embarrassed. They were making such a noise that surely people would be looking at them. But none of the passers-by seemed to mind, or even notice.

People are so free here, thought Tara. They haven't got any respect for anything or anyone. They can do anything they feel like. It was an odd feeling, sort of attractive and exciting in one way, but frightening in another, as if things might suddenly get out of control.

"Tara," said Teriska Khan, breaking in on her thoughts as they started walking back. "You'll have to help me when we get back to the flat. I wouldn't dream of saying a word to Latif, but we'll have to give the kitchen a thorough clean before we start cooking. It's just as well we're here. He needs a family to look after him, poor boy."

26

Autumn, 1985

It was quiet in the school office. The secretary had welcomed Tara and Teriska Khan with an abstract smile.

"Your mother doesn't need to wait," she said. "Tell her she can go home now."

Three months of intensive English at the language school had done its work. Tara understood most things now. She turned to her mother.

"She says you'd better go, Daya."

"Oh."

Teriska Khan looked round the office. The big timetable pinned to the wall, the well-tended pot plants, the electric clock ticking quietly over the door and the efficient clack of the secretary's typewriter gave a reassuring impression of order. She picked up her handbag and started towards the door.

"You know where the bus stop is, don't you Daya?" said Tara anxiously. "It's only three stops. Don't get off at the wrong place."

"Of course I won't," said Teriska Khan, trying to sound dignified. "And don't you get lost coming home."

They smiled at each other uncertainly.

When the door had shut behind her, Tara sat down to wait.

"I'll send someone across to take you to your class," the Deputy Head had said when she'd looked out Tara's file and checked on all her details.

The clock ticked steadily on. The office was pleasantly light and airy. Tara allowed herself to relax a bit. She hadn't slept a wink all night. She'd had terrible dreams of stern teachers demanding crossly why she couldn't understand, why her English was so full of mistakes, why she seemed to have forgotten all the Maths and Science she'd ever been taught. It seemed a lifetime ago since she'd sat in a classroom, listening to a teacher, copying from a blackboard. She was sure she'd never be able to understand a thing anyone said to her, or read a word in an English textbook, or write a single sentence without making hundreds of mistakes.

But now she was actually here her confidence was returning. She'd always been near the top of the class at home. Given time and a lot of hard work she'd do the same again, even if it killed her.

The minute hand on the clock clicked onto the hour and at once a deafening bell shrilled out. The secretary looked up and smiled.

"Awful, isn't it?" she said. "You get used to it after a while. It doesn't bother me any more."

Tara could hardly hear what she was saying. As

soon as the bell had stopped ringing, a door somewhere near by had crashed open. Now, outside in the corridor, there was a noise of shouting and trampling feet. It sounded as if a riot had broken out.

Tara looked nervously towards the secretary. Rowdy behaviour would have been instantly and severely punished in any school at home. Surely something awful was about to happen? But the secretary wasn't taking any notice. She was unconcernedly rifling through a heap of papers on her desk.

The door to the office burst open. A young teacher came in. He was dressed in a tracksuit and carried a football under his arm. He took no notice of Tara but perched on the secretary's desk and began laughing and chatting with her.

He had left the door open, and Tara was able to see down the long length of the corridor. The confidence that had been slowly creeping back ebbed right away. She couldn't believe her eyes. This didn't look like a school. It looked like a – like a – she couldn't say what. She had nothing to compare it with. She'd never been in such a place before.

The school children were dawdling from one class to the next. A knot of big girls were laughing noisily and pushing at each other. They didn't look like schoolgirls at all. Most wore something vaguely recognisable as the school uniform of navy skirts and white tops, but one or two were in completely different clothes and even those wearing uniform had such a variety of brightly coloured bags and odd jackets slung over their shoulders that they could have been wearing anything. Behind them came a couple of wrestling boys, one with his head pinned under the other's arm. A teacher, coming from the other direction, was being hailed by half a dozen loud voices.

"Miss! Where's the rehearsal today?"

"Miss, I can't come. I've got the dentist."

"I gave my book to Simon to give you, Miss. Did he?"

Tara wanted to turn tail and run, back to Daya, back to the tiny new house she had to learn to call home, anywhere in fact as long as it was away from here. She'd never felt so alone in her life.

The corridor was beginning to empty when at last a girl came into the office. She had sandy hair and her friendly face was freckled. She was a couple of inches shorter than Tara.

"Hi," she said. "Are you the new girl?"

"Yes," said Tara shyly.

"I'm Vicky," the girl said, smiling. "Miss Hammond said to bring you straight over to the Science block. You're going to be in our class. I hope you've got your running shoes. It's miles and miles to the chemistry lab."

Tara looked doubtfully at her feet. She didn't quite understand. Vicky was half way out of the office already. Tara followed her.

"Your name's Tara, isn't it?" said Vicky.

Tara nodded.

Vicky gave up asking questions. She started

walking a bit faster. Tara hurried to keep up with her. If she lost sight of Vicky her one lifeline in this terrifying place would go.

"Hey! Vicky!"

Vicky turned round. Another girl was running to catch up with them.

"Hi, Sarah."

The other girl looked curiously at Tara.

"This is Tara," said Vicky. "She's the new girl. From the Middle East."

"Oh yes?" said Sarah brightly. "There's another Arab girl in 9L."

Tara cleared her throat again.

"I'm not . . ." she began.

They both turned towards her expectantly.

"I'm not Arab. I'm a Kurd," said Tara.

"You what?" said Sarah.

"Kurdish," said Tara desperately.

"Oh."

Sarah and Vicky exchanged puzzled looks.

The school had been built over and added onto so many times that it was a rabbit warren of stairs, corridors and extensions. To get to the Science block Vicky and Tara had to go down a flight of stairs, through the Art department, past Home Economics and down the corridor that ran alongside the big new sports' hall. They were just coming up to the sports' hall as the P.E. teacher was setting up the equipment with the older boys. There were two sudden tremendous echoing bangs as he slammed the big metal fire doors shut. At the same time the horse, being dragged across the floor, made a deep rumbling noise, while the parallel bars were pulled out from the wall, rattling noisily in staccato bursts of sound.

Tara stopped. Her head was suddenly in a turmoil of terror. Her heart pounded and she cowered instinctively against the wall. Vicky and Sarah walked on for a moment, then realized they'd left her behind and looked back.

"You all right, Tara?" said Vicky. Tara had gone white and she was trembling.

"That noise," said Tara. "I thought . . ."

Vicky laughed.

"Oh, it's always like that when Mr Fry's in there," she said. She paused, obviously expecting Tara to say something.

"I'm sorry," said Tara, recovering with an effort. "I thought . . . it sounds like . . ."

"Sounds like world war three," said Sarah. "Come on, we'll be late, and Miss Hammond'll look at me and she'll turn round and say 'Late again, Sarah. What am I going to do with you?'"

Vicky was still looking at Tara.

"What *did* you think?" she said.

Tara swallowed.

"I got a fright," she said, feeling stupid. "It was like bombs."

"Yeah." Vicky wrinkled her nose in thought. "Have you been in a war then?"

"Yes."

"What, really? With bombs and dead bodies and everything?"

"Yes."

"Wow."

"Hey, did you see *War Games* last night?" said Sarah. "There was this really funny bit where this officer goes up to this prisoner and he says . . ."

They had reached the door of the Chemistry lab.

"Shut up, Sarah," said Vicky, and opened the door.

Tara's first view of her new classmates was not encouraging. She had unconsciously expected something like her old school at home — neat rows of desks, quiet girls with their books open in front of them, a teacher, chalk in hand, presiding from a raised dais.

Instead she saw seemingly random clusters of boys and girls sitting and standing round tables in different parts of the room. There was a cheerful buzz of chatter which died down a bit as they all looked towards the opening door.

Tara looked round the room for the teacher. There didn't seem to be one here. Vicky went across to the biggest group by the window. In the middle of it was a young woman in a pink sweatshirt who was fitting two bits of apparatus together. She seemed too young and casually dressed to be a teacher. She looked up as Vicky approached and saw Sarah, who was trying unsuccessfully to make herself invisible.

"Ah, there you are, Sarah," she said. "Late again. What am I going to do with you?"

Then she saw Tara and smiled. The smile made her look younger than ever.

"Hello," she said. "You must be Tara. I'll come and see to you in a minute when I've sorted this lot out. Sit over there, next to Sharifah, will you?"

The Muslim name startled Tara. She turned round and saw a dark-eyed girl with a long plait of black hair who was absorbed in a book. Tara sat down beside her. Sharifah looked up and smiled fleetingly then went back to her book again. Tara was longing to ask her a question, but Sharifah looked as if she was really concentrating, and anyway, even though everyone else was talking she didn't feel she should. She'd learned the habit of absolute silence in the classroom at home.

"Excuse me," she said at last, plucking up her courage. "Are you Muslim?"

Sharifah looked up.

"Yes," she said shortly. It was clearly not something she wished to discuss. She was about to go back to her book when she caught Tara's eye. She hadn't looked at her properly before.

"Where do you come from?" she said.

"Iraq," said Tara.

Sharifah nodded understandingly, and Tara read an unspoken message of fellow feeling in her face. She felt a little less lonely.

"Class, get out your exercise books, and draw up a graph to show the results of the experiment," called out Miss Hammond.

Tara looked round anxiously. She had no idea what to do.

"Don't worry," said Sharifah, moving her chair

271

closer to Tara's. "I'll get you a book from her, and you can borrow my spare ruler. I'll show you what we've been doing."

27

Tara put her hand in her pocket and pulled out some change. She counted it and sighed with relief. There'd be enough to pay for the bus fare home today, so she wouldn't have to walk.

It was funny, she thought, how your ideas about money changed when you didn't have much. At home in Iraq there'd always been plenty, and she'd spent it for fun, on extra clothes, or sweets, or drinks. But now, when they had so little to live on, every coin was hoarded, and money wasn't for having fun with any more. It was for protection, against hunger, and cold, and having to walk home for miles and miles instead of getting the bus.

The bus came, and Tara pushed past the full seats to an empty one. She was quite tired this morning. She'd been out baby-sitting last night for a Lebanese family who lived nearby. Baby-sitting didn't pay very much, but it was better than nothing. She'd wanted to get a job for ages. Vicky and Sarah both worked in a cafe two nights a week, but Baba wouldn't hear of her doing anything like that, where she'd be meeting strangers all the time, and would have to come home late on her own.

He'd looked upset when she'd said she wanted to work.

"Why?" he'd said. "Don't you get enough food from your own home? Don't I do enough for you?"

Tara had felt terrible. Nearly all the money from the sale of the house in Sulaimaniya had been spent now, and the rest was being carefully hoarded for emergencies. Baba worked at a horrible job in a hospital laundry, where the hours were long and the pay was hardly enough to keep one person alive, never mind a family. And in the evenings he sat with a book, trying to study English, until his eyelids drooped and he fell asleep. Only one thing could ever bring back the energy in his voice and the sparkle in his eyes, and that was news of Ashti.

News came very, very seldom, but it did come. Every now and then the phone would ring, and one of the big network of Kurds in London would have heard from a friend, who'd had a letter from his brother, who'd just got out of Iraq, and had seen Rostam and his nephew alive and well and carrying on the fight.

There'd been terrible nail-biting moments when Baba's big radio, which could pick up programmes in Arabic from all over the Middle East, reported a particularly horrible bombing in the Kurdish areas, or a major battle for a Kurdish town or village. Weeks would pass, and then another message would filter through, that so and so had seen somebody, who'd seen this person or that person, who'd heard that Ashti was all right.

Only last week Rezgar had phoned from Paris to say that he'd heard that Ashti was planning to come out, that he had some contacts who would help him slip through the net that had caught his family and put them in the refugee camps. He'd try to come straight through to Teheran, and Uncle Daban would help to get him out to London.

It had all sounded too good to be true, like just another example of Rezgar's optimism. He'd raised the family's hopes before, and Tara didn't want to be disappointed again. She pushed the thought out of her mind and tried to think about next term.

She was determined, desperate in fact, to do well in her GCSEs, to get decent marks. She wanted most of all to stay on at school and do A level, in Maths at least. If Baba got the well-paid job he was after in Mayfair, in the household of a Saudi Prince, he'd be able to afford to keep her at school. If not, she'd take the Careers teacher's advice and try for a trainee position in a bank or an insurance company. She'd be earning money at once then, and still be learning, and she could always go to college in the evenings, and go on studying, even if it took twice as long. Somehow or other she'd go on with her education.

"Lucky Hero," she thought. "It'll be much easier for her."

She'd been amazed at how quickly Hero had learned to speak English. She sounded just like an English child, and now she'd started school she could even read a few words of English and write her name. Tara envied her sometimes, but not for long. It was depressing to think that she couldn't remember Kurdistan at all, and would be more English than Kurdish when she grew up.

The bus stopped, and Tara got off. She was looking forward to getting home to a good hot supper, to a chat with Daya, a few hours of homework and a bit of time in front of the TV before she went to bed.

It was an ordinary evening at home, like any other, except that Rezgar phoned again.

"What did he say?" said Teriska Khan anxiously when Baba had out the phone down.

"Not much," said Kak Soran. "You know what Rezgar's like. He always exaggerates. He says there's been a lot more fighting — as if we didn't know that already. He's trying to make me believe that Ashti's already on his way to Teheran. He's not *sure*, of course. Rezgar's never *sure*. But he's heard something from someone who met someone — you know what he's like. I won't believe a word of it till I hear from Daban or Ashti himself."

Teriska Khan's face fell.

"You were on the phone for so long," she said. "I did think, this time . . ."

"Well, don't think," said Kak Soran, speaking more roughly than usual. "Don't hope for anything until Ashti walks in through that door."

Tara went to bed early. Her parents were restless and scratchy, and anyway she was tired. She didn't hear the telephone ring, at two in the morning. She heard nothing until her shoulder was violently shaken.

"Wh . . . what . . ." she said, starting up.

Teriska Khan was standing by her bed, holding back her long hair with one shaking hand.

"Daban's just phoned from Teheran!" she said incoherently. "Ashti's out, came out safe into Iran, and he's got right through to Teheran. He's got a small leg wound, but it's not serious, Daban says. He's putting him on a plane tomorrow! Ashti will be here tomorrow! He spoke to us himself! We heard his voice!"

"Teriska!" Tara heard Kak Soran call.

"Coming!" shouted Teriska Khan joyfully, and she ran out of the room.

Tara lay still, her eyes open, looking up at the grey light that filtered through the thin curtains. There was no point in trying to go back to sleep.

"Ashti," she said experimentally. She was thrilled, of course, and happy, and relieved, but she felt a bit nervous too. She hadn't seen Ashti for three years. What would he be like now? And what would he think of his family, of the way they were living here in this little English house, and Dad doing a job he hated, and herself going to school with people like Sharifah and Vicky and Sarah, the sort of girls he'd never met before in his life, and Hero who spoke English better than any of them and even talked in Kurdish with an English accent?

She tried to remember what Ashti looked like. It wasn't easy. She tried to picture him going off to school in his uniform, then at home, talking to Rostam on the blue chairs in the sitting room, and dressed as a pesh murga in the mountains. Nothing seemed very clear any more.

I'm forgetting home. I'm forgetting Kurdistan, she thought sleepily, shutting her eyes. Then, when she'd stopped trying, clear, dream-like pictures began to drift into her mind.

She saw troupes of laughing girls running down a hillside, their rainbow dresses billowing out in the wind like giant flowers. She saw lean, turbaned shepherds leading their lambs through pastures spangled with flowers near a bubbling spring. She saw wrinkled old grandmothers with children all around them, sitting and laughing in a courtyard, listening to Baji Rezan whose restless hands shaped in the air the characters of her unfolding story. She saw a cluster of boys in crisp white shirts, reading a paper near a mosque wall.

The dream was moving too fast now. She couldn't control it any longer. The girls seemed to rise in the air and were blown away on the wind. The sheep and the shepherds scattered as an explosion ripped into the hillside. The old women choked and gasped for breath as a cloud of poisonous gas engulfed them. The boys raised their arms together as the piece of white paper fluttered to the ground. They dropped to their knees, and kissed the dust, the dust of Kurdistan, as a stain of blood spread out from under them, and a crow took off from a tree and flapped down to hover above them.

Then, as Tara tossed and turned in her sleep, a figure marched out of a pair of giant gates that barred the way to the mountains. Ashti, limping a little, came and stood with his family, and the Kurdistan of Tara's dream rolled itself up like a blanket and disappeared.

"We're Kurdistan, you and me, and Baba and Daya and Hero," said Ashti. "Where we are, it is. Kurdistan is its people and they can't take it away from us, even if they lock us out of our homeland and throw away the key."